FRANKIE AND JOHNNY

LET THE MUSIC PLAY

XIO AXELROD

To the lovers, the dreamers, the music-makers.

1

W hat would you call friends who take long walks together, hang out two or three afternoons a week, and occasionally kiss each other goodbye? On the lips, mind you.

Friends with *benefit*? I'd sure like to pluralize that word but, whatever the term is, it describes John Burton and me.

Ever since he breezed into my life this past spring, disappeared without a trace over the summer, and magically rematerialized just as the air turned crisp, I've felt this buzzing under my skin. It's neither pleasant nor unpleasant, but it is unending. And unsettling. And kind of wonderful.

Being with John is like standing at the edge of a great cliff over-looking clear, turquoise waters. He is breathtaking, and inviting, and I want to dive in. I just don't know whether I'd end up in the warm embrace of his impossibly long arms, or if my heart would smash into bits on some outcropping of rocks that I can't see but know are probably there. It's bloody terrifying.

He makes me feel too much.

Having John live so close to the radio station where I work is a blessing and a curse. We've gotten into the habit of taking lunch together again, checking out the local restaurants and bistros. One afternoon he'll choose, and another I will. It's become our thing. He also comes to the station when I'm on the air and just sits while I work the overnight shift.

Who consistently hangs out with a friend at one in the morning? John, it seems.

"I know you need to be in your own headspace,"he said the first time he asked if he could come by. "I won't bother you, I just like watching you in your natural habitat."

"Like I'm a dolphin?" I had grinned over at him as he sat on the other side of the desk looking gorgeous and rugged and perfect, like a tree I wanted desperately to climb.

Ugh.

Even though we just had lunch together this afternoon, John's here again tonight.

Since the renovation of Studio A is complete, I've moved back into my regular space. The booth is moody-yet-airy and still has that new car smell. John's done a fantastic job with it. The polished wood console curves away from the wall and well into the middle of the room, but there's still plenty of walking space between its edges and the built-in shelves.

Mario has exercised his right as station manager to mount a brand, new flat screen television on the wall opposite the door. I keep it on for John when he's here, with the sound muted. He's fond of home improvement shows. Go figure. He pretends to watch, but most of the time, I catch him looking at me. And, god, I wish I knew what he was thinking when he looks at me the way he is right now.

John's ever-present grin tugs at the corner of the mouth that I now know is softer than petals.

"I think the shiny, black disc goes into the paper sleeve," he says.

I blink and realize there's an LP my left hand, its sleeve in my right. I'm holding them apart like they're allergic to each other, while I've apparently been staring at him for who knows how long.

Have I mentioned how much he unnerves me?

I sleeve the record and spin toward the shelves to put it back, exhaling as slowly and as softly as I can manage.

"I was thinking," John says, as I search the stacks for Prince, as he's next in my queue.

Side note, Prince is infinitely better on vinyl. Trust me in this.

"You're always thinking." I'm grateful my voice isn't as shaky as my knees. I really need to get a handle on this infatuation.

"We've exhausted our dining options around here. Maybe it's time we branch out?"

The relaxed, dulcet tone of his voice slides into my veins like a shot of brandy, warm and comforting. It instantly puts me at ease. Johnny could do radio if he wanted to, easily. I would be a loyal listener.

"Tired of the burgers at Barb and Pete's?" He'd claimed they were his favorite, and I've chosen the place as often as possible. I love seeing him happy. Love the little sound he makes whenever he takes that first bite into his burger. Every time. Low and raspy and close to a moan.

Pinching the jacket for *Sign O' the Times* between two fingers, I ease it off the shelf. It's in mint condition, and I almost don't want to pull the record out of its sleeve. Almost.

I startle when I turn and realize Johnny is right behind me, so close I can smell the mint on his breath. So much for getting a handle on things.

"H-hi," I breathe, mentally calculating how many minutes I have left until the next station identification spot. I slide the album onto the desk and face him.

"Hey." John's eyes are soft, and my cheeks heat.

We've shared about a dozen kisses since he dropped back into my life at my boss - Nicki's - party last month. The kisses have been random and disappointingly chaste in comparison to the heat he unleashed upon me that night. I admit, I'd thought things would progress to something more hot-and-heavy in the time that's passed, but they haven't. John is still tantalizingly out of reach.

It's fucking frustrating, to be honest. I can't figure him out. Even now, when he's staring at my mouth like it's his last meal before a fast.

He smiles. "I want to take you out."

"Somewhere new?" My voice is a little tremulous, but I can't help it. He's so close, and he smells so good, and I want so much.

John leans in and drops his head to my shoulder. "Yeah."

After only a moment's hesitation, I reach a hand up to run it through his hair, something I've been longing to do but hadn't allowed myself yet. I didn't know if I was allowed. Still don't, but it's thick and silky as the pads of my fingers slide along the waves. Well worth the risk of censure.

None comes. He sighs under my touch as I graze his scalp with blunt fingernails. The sound he makes is almost a purr.

I am a little overwhelmed, being this close to him. The air between us is pregnant with something I'm afraid to name. What is this? What am I to him?

"What are we doing here, John-boy?"

I really hadn't meant to ask. Not really. Not out loud, because it sounds like a complaint and I have nothing to complain about.

Things have been good between us. Strange and confusing, but good. We talk a lot about everything. Well, almost everything. There's been a sort of unspoken rule that I won't ask him about his life before he moved here. That I won't ask him about *this*, whatever this is between us.

"I was thinking," he says, ignoring my question as he nuzzles into my neck. I fight off a shiver. "I want to take you to dinner in the city. Do you have a place you like? Or one you want to try?"

His words wash over my skin on warm breaths, and it takes a moment for my brain to process them.

"Dinner?" Both of my hands are in his hair now, and I press my nose into it. He smells like heaven. But he said dinner. Not lunch, dinner. That's a whole new kettle of fish. "Like, an evening meal? Together?"

"Yeah." Johnny lifts his head and bends his knees, meets my eyes. I could drown in his, and I do for a moment.

"I...I'm confused," I admit, my voice barely above a whisper. I drop my arms to my sides. I can't think straight when he's around and, apparently, touching him makes it worse. Better. Worse. Whatever.

"Me too," John confesses, surprising me. Amber eyes narrowing, he searches my face.

I wish I knew what he wanted or needed, I'd give it to him in a heartbeat. I'd give him anything he asked, I'm so wrapped up in him.

Maybe he sees some of that because he's practically staring into me, as tendrils of fire lick up my spine.

I let him see. As terrified as I am of letting him know how deep he has burrowed under my skin, if there's any possibility of us becoming something, I can't hide from it.

I have no idea how long we stay like that, caught up in each other's gaze, but the fading verse of Soul Coughing's *Lazy Bones* jars me from the trance. I step around his big body and reach the console just in time to trigger the station ident spot.

Yes, I could automate this procedure. I could automate my entire set. Program in all of the tracks that I want to play, add the required ID segments, and sit on my arse and watch telly. I could ignore my listeners as so many modern jockeys do. But I don't. I can't. I need to feel the flow of my set. Control it. Change it if and when and however I want. It's one of the luxuries that spinning on the overnight shift has afforded me. I mean, Nicki lets me do pretty much whatever I want, and I relish the freedom. Tonight, I wish I'd just pre-programmed everything. This moment between John and me seems enormous. Unprecedented.

"Sorry," Johnny darts back over to his side of the desk. "I didn't mean to get in the way."

"S'alright," I hurry to assure him. "No harm done."

We're silent as I queue up the next song. I'm torn between which Prince track I want to play, but I start the set with Meshell Ndegeocello to buy time to decide.

"So, about dinner..."

I look up and find Johnny watching me. Waiting.

"Dinner would be good," I say with as much reserve as I can muster. Meanwhile, my heart is hammering in my chest. I am trying so hard not to read anything into this.

"Really?" He looks so hopeful it startles a laugh out of me. As if I'd ever say no.

"O'course." I smile at him. "There are a ton of new places I haven't tried. Did you have something specific in mind?"

"I want to take you somewhere you've been dying to go. Or to a place you really love." There's a layer of depth to his voice I haven't heard before.

I want to take you. It's the second time he's said that and when I realize it, I break out in gooseflesh.

I lower my eyes and pick up the Prince, very carefully because my fingers are suddenly clumsy. "There's a place in Midtown that I've heard a lot about but haven't tried."

"Is that in Center City?"

"Yeah, on Thirteenth and Sansom," I reply, blowing a speck of imaginary dust off the vinyl to stop myself from looking at him.

The record really is in magnificent shape. It's more than thirty years old, almost as old as I am, but with much less wear and tear.

"Would Saturday work for you?" Johnny gets up from his chair to lean atop the monitors. I look up as he looks down at me expectantly, a playful smile tugging at his lips.

Once again, I feel like I'm missing a huge part of this conversation. Or maybe I'm just afraid to hope it means what I think it means. After months of wishful thinking, I'm wary.

"Sure." I manage a shrug and return to my task. "Saturday works."

"It's a date, then," he says, softly.

My gaze pops back up to his, and my stupid heart takes off on a gallop. I have to swallow twice before I can speak. "A...date?"

The slow, sinful smile that spreads across his lickable mouth makes me want to vault over the desk and tackle him to the ground. Holy fuck. And hello there, new facet of John I've never met.

"A date, Frankie." He tilts his head to regard me. "I think it's about time. Don't you?"

I honestly haven't a clue what to say.

"Earth to Frankie," his grin is infectious.

"Dyer says the edamame dumplings are, and I quote, orgasmic," I offer out of nowhere. Johnny arches an eyebrow, amused. "At the restaurant. Sampan, it's called."

He blinks languidly. "Orgasmic, hmm?"

I nod mutely, staring up into his fathomless, liquid eyes and try not to combust from the way that freaking word sounds in his rumbling timbre.

And then.

And *then*, Johnny leans over and kisses me. It's slow and sweet and almost makes me miss my next cue, but I wouldn't have stopped if he hadn't pulled away. He hasn't kissed me like that since Nicki's. It had been so long I was beginning to think I'd imagined it. Now, my lips tingle. Bloody hell, *all* of me tingles.

"Work," he commands, chuckling at my expense. I think he quite enjoys keeping me on my toes.

I gingerly lift the needle from the record and place it in another spot. *The Ballad of Dorothy Parker* had been set to go, but there's an even better soundtrack for this moment.

I smirk when Johnny's eyes meet mine. A wide grin spreads across his face while we listen to Prince's flawless falsetto croon *If I Was Your Girlfriend* over one of the nastiest grooves ever recorded.

2

I've fussed around a bit, trying to get ready for my date with Johnny. I don't know why I'm so nervous, except that I have no idea what's going on between us. Do platonic friends who occasionally kiss go on dates?

I realize I'm trying to manage my expectations here. He kissed me, really kissed me - kissed the *hell* out of me - and asked me out to dinner. I'm not stupid. Not entirely. And I'm not so full of self-loathing that I don't recognize when a man is interested in me.

John Burton wants something from me. I just wish I knew what that was. I'd give it to him, I'm sure, regardless.

You see, there are times when I feel like I'm an experiment for him. Like he's using me to test waters he's been afraid to swim in for whatever reason. Other times it's like he's simply easing his way into something. Like he's been comfortable in the pool but is ready to step into the ocean.

I know John was married to a woman, and that the marriage lasted for at least a few years. They'd met at university, from what I could glean from the wee bit of information he's given me. I don't know why they split or anything else about them. I do know there are shadows behind his eyes whenever it comes up in conversation, just before he inevitably changes the subject.

Digging further never feels right. After our nightly chats became a regular thing, I'd looked him up once on social media - with no real results - and had felt guilty about it for a month. I want to know everything about him, but I want him to tell me when he's ready. I hope he gets there with me.

Sampan is busy when I arrive, and I get there first by design. I want to get settled at the table and have a good, stiff drink in my hand before John arrives. I order a shot of Bullet Rye, with a local IPA, and sit so that I have a clear sightline to the door.

John walks in right after I take my first sip of the beer.

Any other time, I would signal my dining partner to let them know where I was. I don't wave to John. Instead, I watch as he stands behind another couple waiting to be seated.

He towers over them. The lighting is dark, and I can only see his head and the top of his shoulders, but John waits patiently as the other couple follows the hostess to their table.

Now I can see him fully. He's wearing a crisp, light-colored button-down under a brown bomber, and dark-rinse jeans. Jesus, Joseph, and Mary, the man is delectable. His thick hair curls at the nape of his neck, and my fingers itch to comb through it again. I've had dreams about that, ever since the night at the station when he asked me out. On our first date. Which is tonight. Right now.

Fuck.

'Our first date', as if there will be more. Will there be? Again, I'm left with to question *what the fuck is happening here?*

Breathe, Franklin. Just breathe.

John is at the podium now. I watch him inquire about our reservation. The hostess smiles and nods, lifting her hand to point in my direction. He catches me staring at him because I'd been too caught up in it to pretend otherwise. The wattage in his smile doubles, and he keeps his eyes in mine as he crosses the room.

I'm peripherally aware of the heads turning and the looks that trail his trip toward me, but my focus is entirely on him. I can't help but stare, the man is gorgeous. And I'm a little tongue-tied when he leans down and leaves a soft kiss on my cheek before he sits in the chair across from me. A light vapor trail of cedar and citrus stretches out between us as he pulls away.

"You look great," he says, admiring my thin, peridot-green sweater. I've paired it with a soft pair of black corduroys that he hasn't seen yet, but I thank him for the compliment.

"So do you," I say. Or, rather, croak. The realization of what we're doing suddenly hits me again. Pterodactyls take up residence in my gut.

John hangs his jacket on the back of his chair.

"Something to drink?"

I raise a shaky hand to beckon the waiter before John has has a chance to answer, even though I know his answer is yes. He's oozing confidence, but there's a tightness in his shoulders that tells me he's nervous too.

"Good evening, gentlemen, are we in need of a drink menu?"

Our waiter introduces himself as Ward, and Ward is, in a word, stunning. Thin as a reed, with flaming red hair and the most adorable freckles across the expanse of his hennaed cheeks. His eyes are a startling green, and I can tell by the way he flashes that blinding, white smile and brushes his loose curls out of his face that he's used to being admired. Probably pays his rent in tips alone.

He eyes John like a medium-rare steak, but he seems oblivious.

"I can help you make your selections, though I have to warn you. I love everything on the menu." Ward's smirk is sexy. Practiced.

John finally turns his attention away from me and up to our overly enthusiastic server. He has a smile for the man, but it isn't the one he'd just given to me.

Something inside me unknots and I relax into my chair. Could be the two ounces of rye I've just slammed, or it could be the man sitting across from me. My guess is that it's a combo. A heady one, at that.

"I'll have one of those," he says, pointing to my half-empty beer. "And another for my date."

I almost choke on the sip of water I'm taking.

"Are you okay?" John asks, as our waiter scurries off to get our drinks. He's up and out of his chair before I can answer, rubbing my back in slow, firm circles.

"M'fine," I manage, reaching again for my glass of water.

I'm grateful the tables on either side of us are still empty - how embarrassing! - but I'm stuck on that word. Date. I mean, I know we'd called it that, but it shocks me to hear John just put it out in the universe that way.

Like he's staking a claim. Establishing his unavailability to the flirty, pretty Ward. The thought warms me.

"I'm set," I repeat, sounding more like myself.

John returns to his seat, concern still etched in his chiseled features.

"Went down the wrong pipe?" He's studying me.

I nod. "Yeah. You just... I mean, I didn't expect you to say that."

"Say what?" His eyebrows knit.

"You called me your date."

Oh, God. That sinful smile slides back across his face. "Well...you are, aren't you?"

"Is that what you want me to be?"

Yes, it's a stupid question but I need some answers. I need to know what's going through that enigmatic head of his.

John takes a deep breath and sits back in his chair. "Okay," he says.

"Okay?"

"You must think I'm really fucking weird." He's smiling, despite the uncertainty in his eyes.

"A little." I grin.

He returns it. "This is very...new to me."

"Dating?"

He drops his eyes to the table. "Dating men."

Oh.

Oh! Right. I'm an idiot.

John peeks up at me from under thick lashes, and I'm filled with such compassion for him, such pride in him that I'm momentarily unable to catch my breath.

"I see," is all I can manage.

"This is a long series of firsts for me," he says, his voice quiet.

He picks up the bottle of beer that Ward sets in front of him before giving me my second.

"Thank you," I murmur to our server, my mind still processing the significance of this evening.

"Are you ready to order?" Ward asks. "Or do you need a couple of minutes?"

"A few minutes." I look to John for confirmation.

He nods and picks up his menu. I don't miss the tremor in his fingers.

After Ward leaves us, I reach across the table and touch John's hand. I want to cover it, but his are so damned large, I'd need both of mine. Which would be awkward at this tiny table, so I just squeeze his fingers and let go.

He lets out a sigh that melts my heart.

Jesus Christ, I am in trouble. In real, actual danger of losing brain cells over this man. I shove that very real fear aside to give him my support.

"You're good people, Franklin Llewellyn."

His eyes are locked on mine, and I can't look away. Don't want to.

"You're not so bad yourself, John Burton."

We share a smile, and it feels like a secret between us. The room fills up rapidly around us, its dark walnut tables wobbling under the weight of glasses, dishes, and errant elbows. On the other side of the slotted partition, the bar teems with hipsters. It's getting noisy in here.

There's a conversation to be had, but this isn't the place for it, and we come to a silent agreement to shelve it for later.

"What's good?" John asks, looking over the tiny-but-extensive menu. "Aside from the orgasmic dumplings, that is."

I scan the menu. "Dyer recommended we do the chef's tasting."

"Ah, we wouldn't have to choose from this crazy menu?" He looks pleased by the notion.

"The chef would choose for us," I confirm. "And we'd get to try a bit of everything. We just need to tell them about any food allergies."

"No allergies. That sounds perfect." John leans back in his chair and takes a swig of his beer.

"I hope you're hungry. I'm told it's a lot of food."

I've had my eye on the short ribs ever since Dyer suggested this place. My focus is on the Big Plates section of the menu until John's voice rumbles across the table.

"I'm starving."

I look up and... Well... The expression on his face, the sultry tone of his voice, they tell me John isn't only talking about the food.

Jesus

I may not survive this night.

3

There's something about autumn in this city. After the often-crushing humidity of summer, fall in Philadelphia is crisp, like a ripe apple you can't wait to sink your teeth into. The leaves have all given up their green for gold, red, and vibrant rust, and soon they'll blanket the sidewalks.

There's only a smattering of trees in my neighborhood, and even those are too young to do more than sprinkle a bit of confetti on the ground, but Bucks County, where the station is – and where John lives - is a fall lover's dream. I enjoy my drive up to New Bromley much more this time of year than at any other. I often head up the interstate to New Hope hours before my shift, just to cruise the winding roads and take in the colors.

"We should go for a drive sometime," I say to John as we stroll through Washington Square. It's a small park in a part of downtown Philly that bustles with commerce during the day but is eerily quiet at night.

Dinner was amazing. The chef at Sampan had sent us dish after dish after tantalizing dish during our tasting. It had gotten to the point where I just couldn't fit any more food in my body. Soft, warm, Cheesesteak bao buns, tender pork potstickers, savory bulgogi, crispy brussel sprouts, kimchee fried rice, the short ribs, and no less than three orders of the edamame dumplings had been washed down with more IPA. It's more than I usually consume in an entire day, and I had struggled.

John had no such problem. I've never seen anyone eat like him. Well, maybe my cousin Roger. But he's Highland stock. Those lads could put away an entire cow and ask for seconds on pudding.

I always take great pleasure in watching John eat. He's a man that really knows how to enjoy food. He'd complimented every dish, making sure that Ward relayed his gratitude to the kitchen.

The chef had come out to see who this person was that had such high praise for his menu. I'd grinned madly, watching John charm the pants off the man.

Now we're walking off our caloric intake, our arms brushing occasionally. I won't lie, I am giddy. Despite being what some might consider a serial monogamist, I've not been on many actual dates.

"No?" John asks when I tell him this.

"I've dated, but I usually end up in a relationship," I say, side-stepping a crack in the slate slab walkway. "And once you're in a relationship, I find that going out on actual dates just doesn't happen."

"It should." There's a note of judgment in his voice.

"I agree, it should."

"I used to take Michelle out when she had the time."

"She's a doctor?" I don't ask. Instead, I state it. I haven't told John that I'd looked him up, but I don't want to hide it either.

John looks down at me, one eyebrow quirked. "An oncologist. Did I tell you this already?"

I duck my eyes. "Uh, no. I...I googled you a while back."

I chance a glance up to his face. He looks pale.

"Don't worry," I assure him. "I didn't find much, you practically don't exist online."

John rubs the back of his neck and winces. "Yeah, I'm not a fan of social media. I prefer to remain anonymous online."

"Very mysterious," I tease. "Are you secretly a spy? Afraid to blow your cover?"

"Yeah, no. Nothing like that. Just private." John doesn't laugh, but he averts his eyes. "Though, I confess, I looked you up too."

This surprises me, though it really shouldn't. Who in the twenty-first century doesn't Google someone after meeting them? And I'm a public figure, of sorts, so there's quite a bit more out there about me to find.

"And?"

"And you're more popular than I thought." He grins at me, shoulders loosening, and we fall back into step. "Did you know you have your own fan group on Facebook?"

I groan. "Yes, I know all about it. Dyer started it as a joke last Christmas, and a few people joined looking for information on the elusive Frankie L."

"A few?" John laughs softly. "There are over three thousand members in there."

"Fuck off," I scoff. "You're taking the piss."

"I'm not!" John's laugh is deep and rich, and his face lights up with his joy, even in the low light of the streetlamps. "If that means I'm pulling your leg, I guarantee you, I'm not. And those three thousand people have a lot to say about you."

I cringe. "I bet."

"They're mostly in awe of you," he says, his voice taking on that honeyed timber he'd had when he asked me out on this date.

I have the sudden image of him pushing me up against one of these ancient trees that surround us and sucking the breath from my lungs. I want to kiss him so badly, I'm itchy.

We reach the middle of the square, and John gestures toward an open bench. We aren't the only ones out tonight. An elderly couple is out walking their toy dog. They give us a wide berth as they pass.

"I'm serious," John continues. "It's what I said to you before, about your relationship with music. People notice. They think you have a gift. Well," he scratches his ear, thinking. "Most of them do. Some believe it's a hoax."

"What is?" I'm watching his mouth as it moves. He hasn't shaved this evening, and his jaw is dusted with a copper shadow. His lips look so damned soft, and I know they are.

"The way you're able to pick just the right song for every caller."

"Oh," I shrug. "That, well…it's no trick, I just know a lot of songs."

John chuckles. "Saying you know a lot of songs is like saying the Pope knows a lot of Catholics. I'm convinced you have music in your veins instead of blood. Have you never played an instrument?"

It's my turn to laugh. "Oh, God. Me with an instrument in my hands? That's been outlawed in, I think, eleven countries."

"Why's that?" John grins and pulls one knee up, turning to face me on the bench. It looks uncomfortable for him, but I don't say anything.

"My hand-eye coordination extends only to me being able to set a needle on a record or flip toggles on a console," I confess. "Really, my attempts to murder the guitar are well-documented. I think Interpol has a file."

John's laugh is decadent and wraps itself around me. His hand comes down on my shoulder, squeezing. For a man who, perhaps, is only now coming out of the closet, he's remarkably comfortable with PDA.

"Aren't you worried?" I ask before I can stop myself.

"About?" His smile twinkles in the ambient light.

"That someone will see you. Us," I add quickly.

John narrows his eyes, his thumb now brushing the nape of my neck. This time, I can't stop the shiver that races down my spine.

"Are you worried?"

"Philly is a fairly tolerant city," I reply. "Especially in this part, but I just meant…"

"I know." He nods to himself before meeting my eyes again. "What was it like, growing up in Scotland?"

"As a gay teen?" He nods again. "It was okay, I guess. Glasgow is a big city. Not Philly-big," I concede. "But big for the UK. Half-a-million people or so."

"Is it diverse?"

"As diverse as Scotland gets." I smirk. "More so now than when I was a lad."

"Did you come out before you moved here or after?"

I have to think about that. "I don't think I was ever *in*. I was a precocious child and my mother had a hard time keeping me out of trouble. When I was old enough to dress myself, she says I didn't give a shit about girls' clothes or boys' clothes, I liked what I liked. She says that was her first clue."

"Was she supportive?" John bites his lip, his eyes sharp as he watches me.

"She let me do what I like. My gran, though..."

Talking about my childhood elicits foreign sensations. That kid is so far removed from who I am now, it feels like I'm talking about someone else.

"It isn't that I had a particularly difficult time of it."

"What about your dad?"

"He and my mom split, and he moved back to Florida when I was three." My thoughts must drift off because John squeezes my knee.

"Sorry if I touched a nerve."

I shake my head, offering him a small smile. "Nah. S'fine. I don't have any scars. It was unremarkable, my childhood. Nothing bad happened, but... I guess nothing particularly good happened either. It was a lot of nothing. Go to school, hang with my mates, part-time job at the chippie..."

He frowns. "The chippie?"

"Fish and chips shop."

"Ah." John grins. "I thought you might have worked in a music venue, or at a local station."

"I was too young and too listless. It took time to figure out how to turn my love of music into a career." I hesitate to share more but fuck it. "I wanted to be a journalist."

John brightens. "Yeah? A music journalist? How cool. You'd be amazing."

I shrug one shoulder, unreasonably pleased. "Maybe. But there isn't much of a demand for them anymore."

"Oh. Yeah, I suppose not." He frowns and we fall silent for a while. John laces our fingers together, and I'm struck anew by how comfortable he seems to be with me.

"You're not anxious about being seen with me?" I lift our hands and drop them. "Like this?"

John starts and then stops, clearly choosing his words. "I spent a long time facing a stranger in the mirror. I didn't want to get to know myself, because I was afraid of what I'd find if I looked too closely. My life was all set, you see. I had the wife, the house. We were going to try for kids," he shrugs. "It was all so pre-determined."

"What changed?" I should let him tell me all this in his own time, but I'm anxious.

"Nothing changed, except maybe my ability to deny the truth. I was unhappy." He sighs and slides his fingers against mine, back and forth. It's hypnotizing. "I met someone, another teacher at the school."

"A man?"

He nods. "Yes. He was out, though not open, so I didn't know right away. It was a small, conservative town. I'm sure he didn't know who he could trust."

John looks at me, and I nod.

"He'd moved out from Boston and was new to the area," he continues. "I struck up a conversation with him in the teacher's lounge on his first day, and we had lunch together just about every day after."

He drops my hand and lifts his to my nape, his fingers curling to cup me. It grounds me in a way I can't explain.

"You made a connection." My voice is breathy, and I lean into his touch.

"Yes, though I didn't see it for what it was, at first. Patrick hadn't come out to me, and I hadn't a clue about myself. Not really. I just loved spending time with him. He made me feel...seen."

"Did you two ever...?" Fuck, I'm so nosy.

John shakes his head. "No, I didn't sleep with him. It wasn't like that."

I mentally kick myself when relief washes over me, but it's quickly followed by a wave of tenderness for this man that knocks the air out of me. My mind supplies Beck as the soundtrack.

If I surrender and I don't fight this wave...

I picture a quiet room until the song fades away and I can concentrate on what John is saying.

"Patrick and I were friends," he continues. I've fallen silent again because I'm trying to be present for him, but he's probably misinterpreting things. His eyes widen. "That's all. But... It was an intense friendship. Michelle and I had other issues. Lots of them, mostly centered around her work hours. I resented how little time I got to spend with her, which is petty, I know. And I knew it at the time, but it didn't stop me from feeling neglected."

John removes his hand from my hair, and I miss the contact. I want to pull him back to me, but I don't. Of course.

"In a way, it was her inaccessibility that led to my self-examination. Well, that and Patrick." John turns to face forward and puts his elbows on his knees, steepling his fingers in thought. "He saw something in me that I hadn't known to look for."

"He knew you were gay? Or...bi?" I sweep my hand over his back in soothing strokes. It's pure instinct, my need to protect him.

John closes his eyes, leaning into my touch. He makes a little sound of pleasure in the back of his throat.

My heart skips a beat or two as a sluice of heat washes over me, and my pants tighten a little around my crotch. I can't help it. I'm drawn to him in every conceivable way. He is so sweet, my teeth hurt. And yet there's such a fire in him, behind his eyes. In his touch.

But listening to him talk about his past, I can hear his pain too.

"One day, after a particularly vicious argument with Shelly, Patrick sat me down in his office. *You have to figure out what's really bothering you,* he said." John exhales sharply. "I didn't know what he meant. *Your complaints are all about time, about how little you get to spend with her, but that's not the issue.* He was so sure."

"What did he think the issue was?"

"Quality. It was about the quality of the time spent with Shelly." John straightens up.

I let my hand drop away and onto my lap, but John surprises me by taking it in his. He laces our fingers together, and a spike of longing goes through me.

John smiles. "Patrick and I, we could talk about anything and everything. I taught English, and he taught physics. It didn't matter. We had so much more in common. Our thirst for learning, our drive to reach the kids under our charge."

I can tell, just listening to him, how much teaching there meant to John. Enough to make me wonder, again, why he'd left it behind. Maybe this Patrick was the reason. If so, I hate him for it.

"Like I said, we'd have lunch and also breakfast sometimes. I ran the debate team, and he'd often sit in on rehearsals after school. We'd sometimes grab a bite to eat afterward."

Huh. "You were dating."

John gives me a weary smile. "Yeah, we were. I didn't know that, of course, but we were. I spent more time with Patrick than I did my own wife."

"But you say it never went as far as..." I hedge. "As an affair?"

"Not a physical one," John squeezes my fingers a little. "We never had sex. Hell, I never even kissed him, but..."

"You wanted to, though?" I ask as delicately as I'm able. "Kiss him, I mean."

John is silent for a few breaths. "Yes," he whispers. "I did." He swallows hard. "I didn't understand it at the time. It wasn't until that night, after the fight with Michelle, when he asked me what I was really pissed about, that I realized I had more of a marriage with him than I did with my wife. I saw him, socially, more than I did the woman I'd pledged my life to. The woman who'd pledged her life to me. Shelly and I were essentially roommates."

"And you were attracted to him," I say, to state the obvious.

"I was."

"Were you still in love with your wife?"

John frowns. "That's the thing, I have no idea. I never saw her. She was always at the hospital. Always. I was lucky if we spent a few hours a week in the same room."

"That's no way to maintain any healthy relationship, much less a marriage."

"Exactly," John agrees. "Don't get me wrong, I understood how busy she'd be, how important her work was, and I was always proud of her. Supportive. I was her number one cheerleader."

"I'm sure you were, but it sounds rather one-sided."

"That's exactly what it was." John sandwiches my hand between his, and it completely disappears.

"Your hands are enormous," I tease, hoping to lighten his mood. "I bet you have a hell of a time finding gloves that fit."

John chuckles. "You have no idea." He bumps my shoulder. "You're easy to talk to."

"I like listening to you." It's a small confession, but his eyes light up with delight.

"Even when I'm telling you about the guy that helped me figure out that I like men too?" He's studying my face, looking for my reaction.

I shrug. "Is Patrick still in your life?"

Just like that, John's expression darkens. I watch, stunned, as his eyes shutter. He loosens his hands around mine, but I clutch one, forcing him to keep the contact.

"No," he says, and the word falls between us like a brick. Topic closed.

Okay, then.

"It was an emotional affair, what he and I had," he continues after a minute or two. "He helped me to figure some stuff out, just by being there." John huffs out a breath. "I'll always be grateful to him for that."

"And since Patrick, have you...experimented with this side of your sexuality?"

"Not much, not really."

"Why not?"

John shrugs. "I don't know, life got in the way. Work. Big changes."

"For eight years?" I am incredulous. I shift on the bench to face him. "John, please, oh *please*, tell me you've had sex in the last eight years."

"Fuck," he laughs. "Yes, of course, I have. I'm not a monk."

"Well, thank fucking God for that," I exhale with relief. That really would have been too much to take.

"I've been with women since Michelle," he says, calming down.

And the penny drops.

"But not with men."

John meets my gaze. "No." He smiles into my eyes. "To be honest, Frankie, I haven't been remotely interested in anyone until recently."

"Oh?" I say, electricity dancing along my tender nerves. "Fancy someone, do ye?"

"Aye." He draws out the word, teasing, and gives me a wink. "I do."

"I see," I say, weak for him.

"Frankie…" My name sounds so good coming out of his mouth in that pleading tone. Like he can't wait to get me alone. Bloody hell.

Why is it suddenly hot out here, has summer returned in the last hour or so? Because the faintly pink streetlights now seem too bright, and I'm roasting in my own skin.

"Maybe we should walk some more." I'm panicking, and my words come fast. Why am I panicking?

"Or…" He lifts a hand to trace a fingertip across my bottom lip.

A shudder passes through me, followed by a lightning bolt of desire that lands right on the tip of my cock. I have never, in my life, responded to anyone the way I respond to John Burton.

"Or," he says again. "You could show me where you live."

Right. That would be the reason for the panic.

4

"It's not much," I say as we step into my flat. "The girls went to a club and won't be home 'til the wee hours."

"You have roommates?" John's eyes scan the living room, which is unusually tidy.

Okay, yes. I'd tidied it up before I left home. Just in case.

My style could be called dormitory chic, my flat furnished with a collection of mismatched pieces acquired over the life of my residency. Some of it, like the tiny kitchen table and chair set, have been here since before I ever arrived. But the parlor has high ceilings, which gives it the impression of space and makes the collection seem eclectic rather than haphazard.

"They sublet the front bedroom from me," I explain, flicking on lights as I go. It takes six lamps to fill the room, one of the downsides of its twelve-foot ceilings. Even with white walls, the light barely reflects. "They do their thing, and I do mine."

"So, not close, then?" John settles on the couch and looks up at me.

"Not at all. Wine?" I offer. "Beer?"

"Beer, if you have an IPA."

"I do." I grin. "Be right back."

The large, overstuffed couch is the primary source for seating. Along the opposite wall is where I keep my personal collection. LPs, CDs, and rare box sets, both vinyl and digital. My Technics turntable occupies the place of honor where a television might sit. I have a telly, but it's in my room. I didn't want to have to argue with the girls, or anyone else, about what to watch.

When I return with two cold bottles of brew, I find John flipping through my record collection.

"I hope you don't mind," he says, reading the back cover of a Police album.

"Not at all," I say. I've never been one of those people that doesn't let others touch their prized possessions. As long as they're gentle, it doesn't bother me.

"You have a lot of eighties music here," John observes. "I guess you weren't kidding about the whole birthright thing."

"I was not." I hand John his beer and take a look at the record in his hand. "God, I love that album." It's *Zenyatta Mondatta*, one of the most underrated albums of that decade.

"I don't think I've heard it," John admits. "The only Police songs I know are *Roxanne* and *Every Breath You Take*, which is super fucking creepy if you ask me."

"Right?" I exclaim. "Totally mental! It's downright stalkerish. *Wherever you go, I'll be watching you.* Really sick shit." I take a pull from my beer as John nods in agreement.

"I think my parents had that as the first dance at their wedding."

"Fuck," I mutter. "Did they not read the lyrics?"

John laughs, his malty breath filling my lungs when I inhale. "I doubt it. My mom had dubious taste in music."

"What were they like, your parents?"

John looks thoughtful for a moment. "Kind," he says. "Not nice, I mean of course they were nice, but being kind is different than being nice. Does that make sense?"

"It does," I reply, recognizing the trait in their son. John is kind. And nice. More than that, he is genuine. "Do you want to hear it?"

"What?" My question brings John back to the present.

I nod toward the album in his hand. "The best fucking record you've never heard."

He grins, handing it to me. "Blow my mind, Frankie."

It takes me no time to cue up the first song, *Don't Stand So Close to Me.*

We talk through most of the track as I explain how the band hated the record and were rushed to get it done it before their next tour.

"Of course, it won two Grammys," I tell him. "Shows what the fuck they knew."

"Yeah, really."

We go quiet as the album progresses, content to be in each other's company, sharing a beer and a sofa. I love this, sharing music like this, and there are few people on the planet with which I can do it.

John really digs the second song, *Driven to Tears.*

"One of my favorite political songs," I tell him.

The following track has one of the fattest grooves I've ever heard on a rock record, but I don't say anything to John when it begins.

"Damn," he says, when the bass line kicks in and looks over at me.

I nod. "I know."

He grins, his expression softening as he studies me.

"Fuck," he exhales the word.

"What?" I ask.

Someone left a bolt of cotton fabric at my place long ago, and it's found new life as a tablecloth, though it actually only covers a diamond-shaped area of the surface. Very shabby chic, the girls tell me. It almost looks like I did it on purpose.

This is what runs through my mind as John puts his bottle on the red and white patterned cloth. He turns to me, pulling his knee up so he can face me.

"What?" I ask again, beginning to squirm under his gaze.

"Nothing, I just..." He exhales slowly and takes my hand. "I really like you, Frankie."

I grin. "I really like you too, Johnny. Wanna go steady?"

I laugh, but John doesn't. "Yeah, I think... I think I kinda do."

He leans forward, pulling me in, and kisses me.

It starts off sweetly enough, but then, holy fuck, he's really going for it. Hot and wet, with just the right amount of pressure to melt my brain.

John moans, and my brain goes all fuzzy. I'm shaking, and my skin feels entirely too hot and too tight. And I'm wearing too many damned clothes.

"Wait," I pant, breaking the kiss. "John, I..."

"Did you not want me to do that?" He asks, but his hand is in my hair, gathering it into his fist. "Or this?"

He pulls me into him and plunders my mouth again.

Fuck, I'm... I'm lost. Euphoric. I can't rub two neurons together to form a coherent thought. I sink a hand into his thick, satiny hair and use the other to grab onto his shoulder.

"A-are you sure?" I'm panting as his lips trail down to my throat. He licks a wet stripe there before making his way back up to my ear where he nibbles on my lobe.

"Frankie, you're all I've thought about for months." John pulls back to meet my eyes. His are nearly black with arousal.

I take in his ravaged lips, his tousled hair, and his hooded eyes. He's so fucking sexy, I can barely breathe.

"If you don't want this, want me..." John hesitates. He's unsure, now, and it's my fault.

"Are you fucking kidding?"

I grab his hand and shove it between my legs to where my dick has transformed into living stone. My heartbeat pulses in its tip, and know I'm already wetting the front of my boxer-briefs.

He runs his open fist along my length, and I slap his hand away, my balls tightening threateningly.

"Don't make me come like this."

John growls. He fucking growls. "How do you want me to make you come, Frankie?"

Christ in Heaven. I want him to fuck me, but I don't think we're ready for that. At least he isn't.

This is when I remember that John's never done this, any of it. Not with a man. I'll be his first for everything. I push him away from me.

He frowns until I bring my leg over his lap and straddle him.

I sit close to his knees to give us both room to explore. Never taking my eyes out of his, I reach forward and slowly unbutton his shirt, entirely aware that my breathing is too shallow and too fast.

John's breath catches, and his eyes go molten with need. He's trembling with it.

"You watch porn?" I ask. I need to steer us toward safer ground.

He meets my eyes, one corner of his mouth lifting into a wicked grin. "Yeah."

"Yeah?"

I'm teasing him now, parting the halves of his shirt to reveal an expanse of smooth, golden skin, lightly dusted with a strawberry blonde thatch. His pectorals are perfect, like a sculpture, and his abs ripple evenly down his torso. He is so goddamned delicious, and I'm eager to taste him. I help him shrug out of the shirt and get my first real look at his powerful arms.

"Wow," is my expert assessment.

The corner of his mouth lifts in a smug grin. He knows he looks good.

"Your turn."

His fingers tug at the hem of my jumper, and I lift my arms to allow him to pull it up and off. Next to go is my tee, and then we're both shirtless. Staring. Panting. Quivering like a pair of virgin teenagers.

Vulnerability looks so sexy on him.

"You're gorgeous," John breathes, leaning forward. He licks a line across one of my nipples. I inhale sharply at the contact.

I've never done as much gasping as I have since I met this man. You'd think I'd never been touched before. I feel the stinging pressure of his teeth on the hardening nub before he sits back, running his hands along my chest and abdomen.

"How can you have a body like this? You don't work out, at least not that I've seen." He's looking at me like I'm the sexiest thing he's ever laid eyes on. It's such a bloody turn-on.

"Genetics." I shrug and lean forward to bury my face in the curve of his neck. I've been dying to do this for months, inhale him like this. Drown in his heat and his scent. In him. "And I do a few crunches every morning."

His hands are on my ass now, kneading it as he pulls me forward. Driving me insane. I can feel the heat of his palms through the fabric and grind down on him. The friction is delicious.

"God bless your parents," he mutters as I nibble on the corded muscle I find on his neck.

"Only bloody thing they ever gave me," I murmur.

"What?" John leans back and looks up at me.

"Nothing." I frame his face in my hands.

"I... I don't have a clue what to do," John says, his voice thick with desire.

Tilting my head, I run my fingers through his hair. He's beautiful like this, skin flush with passion, eyes glistening, lips ravaged.

"Kiss me," I demand.

I don't have to tell him twice.

5

John is fucking adorable.

He kisses like a novice, all wet enthusiasm and unsure hands. A talented novice, because every sweep of John's tongue against mine strips away a little more of my control.

I am painfully hard, and no amount of shifting my position on his lap offers any relief. Precisely the opposite.

We break-off what must be our hundredth kiss, both breathing hard.

John brushes his lips across my cheek, my other cheek, my chin, my forehead, before resting his head on my shoulder. His hands smooth up and down my back, his touch sure and uncertain all at once. They settle on my hips, and he squeezes hard. It feels like being claimed.

The thought leaves me trembling. Needy. My body begins to soften, readying itself to welcome him inside. And yet I'm worried about pushing him too far too fast.

"Tell me about your first time," John whispers into my ear, hoarse and husky.

I startle when what he's actually said reaches my one functioning brain cell.

"Wh-what?"

He rolls his head to plant kisses along my collarbones and throat. "Was it good for you?"

"First times are never anything to write home about, are they?"

"Michelle was my first," he offers. "Neither of us knew what we were doing."

"Sort of goes with the territory, I suppose."

My hands are on his shoulders, kneading them. Sliding into his hair and combing through the tangles.

"I fooled around long before I had actual sex," I tell him.

"Yeah?" He leans back against the couch, putting space between us, but his hands immediately begin to rub up and down my thighs.

It's like he can't stop touching me. I love it.

"I was fifteen, at a party with some mates from school, the first time anyone other than me put their hands on my dick."

"Wow, fifteen?" He looks genuinely surprised, which makes me laugh.

"We're not so uptight in Scotland as you Americans." I smile at him, lifting my hand towards his hair again. I can't stop touching the silky strands. "How old were you when a girl first touched you?"

"Eighteen."

I choke back a laugh. "Eighteen? Christ, man. How'd you get through high school?"

His laugh is sub-sonic. "A lot of self-love." He leans in again.

Kissing John Burton is quickly moving to the top of things I love to do. He does it with his whole being, holding nothing back. He tastes of beer and spices. It's intoxicating.

"What's that sound?" He murmurs into my mouth.

The only thing I hear is my pounding heart, our mingled breaths, and the snick-snick-snick of...

"Shit!"

I scramble off John's lap and rush over to my record player. The needle bumps up against the label of the album before I gently lift it and set it on its cradle. I can't believe I let it run out like that. I can't believe I hadn't noticed when the music stopped. I'm slipping the vinyl back into its sleeve when I feel John's hands on my shoulders.

He lifts my curls and presses a kiss to my nape. "Is it okay?"

"Better than," I assure him, shelving the record and flipping on one of my digital mixes instead.

"You don't like silence, do you?" John's question isn't an admonishment, as it has been for so many others before him.

Few people understand how much I need music around me at all times. I have a disorganized mind, and music gives me something to focus on. Silence is loud. Abrasive. Because there's no such thing as pure silence, not unless you're in some sort of sensory deprivation tank. There's always the hum of a lamp, the clanking of pipes, the rumbling engine of a passing car.

"I sleep with music on," I tell John as the first song begins.

It's *The Eraser* from Thom Yorke, edgy and mellow at the same time. His music has a manic energy to it, even when it's restrained by a minimalist arrangement and sparse vocals

"I shower with music. Eat with it. Everything."

"Really? Everything?" John's hands slide down to my hips, and he pulls me against him.

I lean my head back against his broad chest and breathe in deep, humming on an exhale.

He wraps his arms around me, one across my collar and one around my chest, and it feels so damned good. His hands splay across my skin, sure and possessive.

"Even when I can't have it around me, it's still inside my head. It's a part of me."

"I know this about you," his voice sends goosebumps racing across my skin. There's no judgment or disapproval in his tone, only warmth. Acceptance.

"Ever since I was a child, I've had a theme song for every member of my family, for every room in our house, even the path that I took to school. This flat. It isn't voluntary, really, it just…is."

And it isn't something I've ever shared with anyone else. My parents already thought I was obsessed. If they'd known I couldn't shut the music out, even when I wanted to, they'd have sent me off for analysis.

My mom was big on analysis.

"My da would come into the room at night and turn off my stereo, worried the music would affect my brain, somehow."

"He was probably right, though I don't think that's a negative thing," John squeezes me tighter. I can feel his erection pressing against the small of my back.

I turn in his arms and look up at him.

"You're a bit of alright, you know." I smile as I smooth my hands up his chest, lightly scraping my blunt nails over his skin as I go.

"Do you have a song for me?"

I'm expecting the question, and I wish I had an answer. John inspires so much music in me, but I haven't found *his* song.

"Not yet." I run a hand down his chest and pinch one of his nipples.

He hisses, his eyes narrowing to slits. "What am I going to do with you?"

I slide the hand down to palm his cock through his jeans, and he bucks into it.

"What do you want to do with me?" I feel him throbbing in my palm already, and I can't take it. I need to touch him.

I flick open the button of his jeans and ease the zipper down, watching his expression as I do.

His lips part, his breaths humid bursts across my cheek.

"Frankie…"

"That porn you were going to tell me about?"

"Was I?" He chuckles breathlessly.

"Mmm-hmmm." I slip my hand inside the waistband of his underwear and groan at my first, brief brush of skin against the hard, naked length of him. Jesus.

John makes a sound in the back of his throat that falls somewhere between pleasure and pain.

"What do you like to watch" I coax him into my grasp. "What have you imagined us…me…doing?"

John cries out when I give him a gentle squeeze. His head drops to my shoulder until he's hunched over. It can't be comfortable for him.

I grab onto his hips and shuffle-dance him backward, toward the sofa. When the backs of his knees hit it, I release him, and he tumbles down. I follow and turn him so he's reclining its length, and push his legs wide so I can kneel between them,

John's eyes go molten as I reach for his erection again, his hooded gaze flicking back and forth between my face and the hand I slide around his thick length.

"Tell me what you want, Johnny." I flick my thumb over the head of his cock. He's cut, smooth as silk, and hot as a brand. "What have you imagined me doing?"

"Your mouth," he grinds out, hips moving as he pumps shallowly into my grip.

My dick complains, so I release the button on my cords and lower the zipper to relieve the pressure.

"You've imagined my mouth?" I lick my lips and grin when he groans low and loud.

"Y-yes."

"Doing what?" I stroke him once and then grab the waistband of his jeans and his boxers and pull them down his hips for better access. His balls are heavy and full, and my mouth is watering now.

John's erection is thicker than mine, though shorter. It's glorious, and I can't wait to wrap my lips around it. I inhale his musky scent, tempted to run my tongue along his bare length. But, I'm a cautious little biscuit.

"Be right back," I say, and hurry over to my jacket to fish out my wallet, where I keep a condom or two. I have a whole box in my bathroom, but time is of the essence. My patience is thin.

When I return to John, he's fisting himself and stroking. I bat his hand away.

"Mine," I tease before tearing open the packet. I lean down and roll it onto his length with my mouth in one smooth motion. It's a trick I learned on a banana in secondary school.

His hips piston up from the sofa, and I have to pin him down.

"Holy fuck!" John moans loudly when I engulf the base of his cock, nestling him in the back of my throat. "Jesus, Frankie..."

Loving the way my name sounds in his husky, lust-soaked rumble, I hum around him and draw up to circle the tip with my tongue, glad I picked the rubber with the cherry-flavored lube. I tease the spot just under his crown, and he shudders.

"You need to get tested," I husk as I pull off, pumping him in my fist. "I want to taste you for real."

"Yes." The word flies out of his mouth like a bullet.

I can't get enough of the way John's entire body strains toward me. His legs shake on either side of my hips, the muscles twitching and jumping with every touch. Thick, ropey veins traverse the forearm thrown across his hard, flat stomach. He heaves with every breath he takes, his hands fisting. One in my hair, one against his skin, like he's trying to contain himself.

I want him wild. I want to strip away all of that control.

"You're bloody beautiful," I whisper before sliding him back down my throat. I hollow out my cheeks, drawing on him like he's my last breath. When I tug lightly on his balls, he shudders again. Hard.

"God...damn!" His other hand slides into my hair, and he grabs my head. Not too tightly, but tight enough for me to know he likes what I'm doing to him. "It's good," he groans. "Shit, so fucking good."

I bob up and down, setting a brutal pace. I need to see him lose it, need to feel him come apart underneath me. It's suddenly the most important thing in the world.

"Frankie...fuck, I..."

"Come." I gasp quickly before resuming my punishing pace. My lips are numb around his girth. My jaw aches, but I can't stop. I won't stop.

John lets out a sharp shout, and then I feel him pulsing against my tongue. His entire body ripples like a ribbon in the breeze as he comes and comes, the condom filling fast.

I sit back and watch in awe, my hand still wrapped around him, drawing out every bit of pleasure that I can get from him.

John places his hand over mine to still it, and I eventually release him. He flings his arm over his eyes, his breaths coming quick and hard, and he laughs. It's a delighted, delirious sound.

After gently removing the condom from him and tying it off, I wrap it in a leftover napkin from the Chinese takeaway I'd had earlier in the week. I set it on the floor. I'll deal with it later. Right now, I watch John float back to earth. Me, I'm still as hard as granite. I palm my erection.

John's arms fall to his side. He's blinking up at the ceiling, and he's gone quiet. Too quiet.

"Are you alright?"

"Yeah." John exhales, and his eyes slide down to meet mine.

The smile he gives me is stunning. Beatific. It makes my heart stutter in my chest.

"Come here," he commands, and I rise up to stretch my body over his.

He's so warm, I want to sink into it and never leave, but I brace myself over him. "What's on your mind?" I search his face, my gaze catching on those full lips of his.

"You." John slides his big, warm hands down my chest, around my sides, and down to my ass, where he palms me and pulls me down onto him.

He can't possibly miss how hard I am.

Nope, he hasn't. He moves one hand between us. I inhale sharply when he wraps his fingers around my aching cock.

John must like that reaction because I'm suddenly on my back next to him. He leans over me, resting on his elbow, and searches my face. For what, I don't know. I just don't want him to stop touching me.

"More," I plead. I'm leaking into his hand, making the slide of his grip smooth and slick.

"You said I need to get tested," Johnny says, drawing me out of my pleasurable haze.

"Huh?"

"You said I need to get tested, not you." He continues to stroke me, mercilessly slow.

Does he really think I'm capable of actual thought right now? "Yeah," I manage to say. "You do, so I can-"

"Not you?"

Oh. "I get tested every six months," I pant, squirming. "Last test three weeks ago, though I haven't been...ohgod...I haven't been with anyone in months...John..."

"Yeah?" John slows his strokes to nothing.

"Nooo," I moan. Or whine. "Don't stop. Please."

It takes a moment for me to realize he's moved, no longer face-to-face with me. I look down to find him staring at my dick.

"John, you don't have to." I try hard to keep the abject need for his mouth on me out of my voice. The number of times I've fantasized about this very moment is incalculable. Sad, really.

"You're clean, right?"

I nod. "Yeah, I... Yeah. I can show you, but I have more condoms in-"

"Frankie," John says, raising his eyes to mine. "I trust you." He holds my gaze, and something passes between us that I can't describe.

There's a shift, a change in the air between us. This is the beginning of something. This is where we start.

John lowers his mouth to my dick, his tongue tentatively licking my throbbing, nearly purple head as he gently pulls back my foreskin. At the first gush of his warm breath on me, I buck hard.

"I've never seen an uncut prick before," he says, fascination in his voice.

"N-no?" I manage. I'm propped up on my elbows, staring down the length of my body, as the most beautiful man I've ever seen licks my cock like it's a Chupa Chup.

So surreal.

"It's the same as mine, but different. More skin," John narrates like this is a bloody documentary. "You're longer than I am but a little thinner."

"You don't like it?" I'm so nervous, it's crazy. I'm sixteen all over again, shivering with anticipation in the back seat of Magnus Michaelson's Peugeot.

John peers up at me and grins. "You're kidding, right? You're fucking gorgeous, Frankie. Every inch of you."

"You haven't seen every inch," I remind him.

"Next time," he says, returning to his cock worship. "Right now, I'm occupied with these eight."

When the wet heat of John's mouth surrounds me for the first time, I know that I'm going to embarrass myself. I'm going to come in about three seconds, and there's nothing I can do about it.

"John..."

He lifts his head. "I know, babe. It's okay, this is the first of many. I just want to make you feel good." He licks my length, and I moan, my hips bucking.

He looks so goddamned amazing between my thighs.

"Give me what I want, Frankie," John growls. "Let me drink you down."

Holy shit. I'm gone. I collapse onto the sofa.

He sucks me into his mouth, not quite to the back of his throat, and I'm grabbing the cushions, the throw pillows, anything I can get my hands on.

The tingle starts in the small of my back and travels down to my balls, which draw up so tight I think they might explode.

"Johnny...fuck...John...I can't..."

In response to my pleading, he moans around my dick, and I disintegrate. I'm coming so hard, my vision blurs. There are stars behind my eyes, and a whirring sound in my ears, followed by pounding in my ribcage. Like someone's trying to break through a door that's been bolted shut.

It takes a few seconds for me to realize it's my own heart I'm hearing. Feeling. The aftershocks are relentless as John licks up every drop of my release like a pro.

"Are you sure that was your first time?" I ask when I'm finally able to breathe.

John smiles up at me. He's laced his fingers across my abdomen and has propped his chin on them. He looks ridiculously pleased with himself, which I suppose he should be. I don't think I've come harder. Ever.

"That was incredible," he says as if he's just witnessed the miracle of life. "But, babe, this has to be the most uncomfortable sofa ever. What were you thinking when you bought it?"

He winks.

I laugh. I can't help it. He's just so bloody sweet and sexy and – fuck - I'm in so much trouble.

"I think I picked it up at Top Comfort Furniture," I say, trying to recall.

"Well," he says, kissing his way up my body until he reaches my mouth. He braces himself over me, the muscles of his arms bunching. "So much for truth in advertising."

"My bed is a slice of heaven," I say, still weak but so very happy.

John grins down at me. "Mmmm," he hums. "Lead the way."

6

"Whatever you're on, I want some." Dyer eyes me suspiciously from across the table.

I've been staring off into space, thinking of the only thing I ever seem to think about anymore, aside from music. John Burton.

Dyer and I are at a tiny pizza place on the waterfront that I can't even remember the name of, despite sitting on its patio. The signage here is dismal.

"I feel like we're eating at someone's home, are you sure this is legal?"

"Nice deflection," he says.

It's a warm, sunny afternoon, and Dyer's grey eyes are hidden behind the mirrored surface of his sunglasses. Despite this, I know he's studying me carefully.

"You've been awfully tight-lipped about you and John."

I stick a tortilla chip in my mouth to buy time. Dyer's right, I haven't spoken to him, or anyone, about what's happening between John and me. It's so new and so fragile, I'm feeling overly protective of it.

I've been floating in a bubble, and I don't want it to burst.

"You like him, that much I can tell." Dyer steals a chip from my plate.

"Brilliant powers of deduction there, Watson."

"Don't British at me," he scolds, fanning himself. "You know what that does to me."

"Shut your gob." I throw a chip at him, and he catches it, tossing it into his mouth.

"Okay, that wasn't sexy at all." He grins, dimples popping, and slips off his glasses.

Sometimes I forget how breathtakingly beautiful Dyer is. Like right now. The sun glints in his snowy, blonde hair. His eyes are the same color as the clouds above. His skin has a splash of crimson in it today and is a shade darker, thanks to a long weekend in the Bahamas he'd finagled last week.

He's sitting in a plastic patio chair that has seen better days, but he somehow makes it look like a throne.

Dyer is unreasonably handsome.

"I'll tell you about Johnny if you tell me who took you to the islands last week."

"So," he begins loudly. "How *is* the family back in jolly old England?"

"Scotland," I correct him. "They're good, thanks. Now, who's deflecting? Are you seeing someone? Like, really seeing someone?"

"I'll tell if you tell," he sing-songs.

"Fine," I huff, caving in. Not because he's pressuring me, but because I need to talk it through with someone, and Dyer is as close to a best friend as I've ever had.

He picks up his glass of lemonade, licking the paper straw into his mouth with a long, sinful tongue. It's meant to be obscene, and it is.

I laugh and shake my head. "You're a pig."

Dyer shrugs, completely unapologetic. I love this about him.

"Spill."

"Right." I clear my throat, which is suddenly dry. "Right, so, we've been sorta seeing one another."

"Obvs," Dyer says, feigning boredom before he leans forward to rest his elbows on the table. His eyes dance with mischief. "Get to the good stuff. How big is his dick? It's enormous, isn't it? Wait! Don't tell me, I don't think I could handle him being that hot *and* having a big shlong too."

"Shlong?" I look at him like he's mental because he is.

Dyer waggles his eyebrows. "Does he at least know how to use it? His big fucking dick?"

Naturally, a young mother with her toddler wanders into the area just as those delightful words leave Dyer's mouth. But he flashes his blinding smile, and the woman grins, blushing as she ushers her kidlet into the restaurant.

It's sorcery, really.

"So unfair," I complain.

Dyer waves it off. "Don't get sidetracked by my awesome. Keep talking about your John Bunyan."

"Who?"

"Franklin!"

"Fine." I sit forward and lower my voice.

John's substitute teaching in Newtown today, but I still feel like there are ears everywhere.

"We've been spending a lot of time together, like I said, and it's been...well, it's been fucking incredible."

"I knew it!" Dyer exclaims, slapping his hand on the table. Several birds that had been pecking around the patio for leftovers scatter into the blue sky.

"Will you keep the volume down?" I scold him. "Do you even know the word discreet?"

"I've heard of it," he quips. "Sounds boring, though. So, go on, tell me all about your love affair with the hot contractor."

"We talk. A lot." Dyer scrunches up his nose. "And we make out like first-year uni students."

"Better," he says, leaning in closer.

"And we've....done things, but not the deed. You know?"

Sitting up, Dyer frowns. "Why the fuck not?"

This is the tricky part. I don't want to betray John's confidence, but

I need to talk through my reservations. John hasn't put any pressure on me to go further than we had back at my apartment last Saturday night, but sometimes, when he looks at me, I know exactly what he wants. Because I want it too.

"He hasn't been out of the closet long," I say, hoping it's enough of the truth to make the rest of what I have to say make sense. "And I'm the first guy he's dated."

"No." Dyer's eyes go wide as plates. "Seriously? You got a fucking virgin! A hot fucking virgin?"

"Jesus Christ, Dyer, keep your bloody voice down."

To his credit, he slaps a hand over his mouth. "Sorry, girl. Sorry."

Dyer scoots his chair around the table until he's sitting right next to me. When he speaks again, his voice is quiet. Almost reserved.

"Okay, now I understand the cloak and dagger," he says, patting me on the arm.

"The what?"

"If he's a newborn, and you're his first, he's got to be...skittish about the whole being-seen-in-public thing."

I bristle. "We go out all the time."

"Yes, but not around people, you know. Not with your friends, or his." Dyer pauses. "Does he have any friends? He must, right? Have you met them?"

"No, but then he hasn't met mine either."

"What friends do you have, besides the zoo at 'KMP? And he's met just about everyone there."

I want to protest, but Dyer is right. Just about everyone I care about works at the station.

"Again, I ask you, old friend, is he ready to be coupled-up? In public? Because you've been walking around with your head in the clouds since Nicki's last bash." Dyer tsks and grabs another chip from my plate. "Don't fall for the guy if he's not ready to be out. Hiding is so pre-Obama."

I know Dyer is speaking from experience. His last - and only - serious relationship was with a guy so firmly planted in the closet, he was load-bearing. It had taken being disavowed in a very public, painful way to get Dyer to walk away from the two years he'd invested. He'd earned his right to be a man-whore.

"Are you? Falling in *love*?" He's only half-teasing and shrugs when I wave him off. "Better figure it out soon."

I am not going there. Nerves begin to creep into my John Burton high, so I switch the topic of conversation over to Dyer and his mystery lover.

"Enough about me. Tell me about your trip-buddy." Dyer rolls his lips inward as I eye him, and I can't help but poke at him. "Who are they, anyone I know?"

Dyer's very open about his sexual conquests. I've only ever known him to date someone for a week or two before he gets bored – with that one notable exception. He adores sex and doesn't care who's giving or receiving, or what body parts are involved.

"It's not a big deal," he says, averting his gaze. "Just a little fun."

I narrow my eyes. He's being uncharacteristically stoic about his love life. It's not a word I ever thought I'd use to describe him. If anything, Dyer's usually guilty of over-sharing.

"Hey," I say, nudging his elbow with mine. "You alright?"

He nods and slips his sunglasses back on. "Yeah, all is well in Dyerville."

"Cause you know you can talk to me, right?" I duck my head to meet his eyes, even though they're shaded now. "I'm always here for you."

Dyer turns his head to me and nudges his glasses down his nose to peer over the rims. That silvery gaze is piercing.

"He's going to fall madly in love with you if he hasn't already," he declares. "I wish I'd had the good sense to snatch you up, back when we first met."

I snort. We've each said this to the other at least once, both knowing it would have been a disaster. "We would hate each other by now."

Dyer sighs dramatically. "Yes, you are so right. I could never put up with your music mania. I love music," he says. "You *love* music. It's kinda freaky, actually. And you're a prude."

"Prude or not, you love me," I tease, pushing him in his seat until he almost topples out of it.

"Bitch!" He exclaims, scrambling to his feet just in time.

I laugh. Loudly.

"I hate you," he sneers without venom and then winks at me. "I've gotta skedaddle. Catch you later?"

"Yeah," I reply, gathering our paper plates and napkins from the table. "I guess I'm on clean-up duty."

"Dyer doesn't do domestic," he deadpans before he spins in his rainbow Chuck Taylors and scurries off.

***

"Guess what?" John asks when I open the door for him.

He's a little late getting to the studio tonight. I wasn't sure he was coming at all until I got his text saying he was on the way.

"What?"

He plants a quick kiss on my cheek as he walks by me.

I follow him back to the booth, where I'd been in the middle of setting up my next block of songs. My mood has improved dramatically since he told me he was coming, and I'm smiling already.

John grabs the television remote from the side of the desk and turns the set on, muting the volume.

I look up at the screen, and my smile widens. "Purple Rain!"

John beams at me. "Yep. I saw a commercial for it after work today and figured we could watch it during your shift."

"That's a perfect plan," I agree.

He looks pleased. Happy. We hold eye contact for several breaths, the air charged between us.

Shaking my head, I turn my mind back to work. "Hang on, take these."

I hand over a pair of headphones.

"What's this for?" He eyes them, confused.

"Plug them into the TV so you can hear the film."

"Oh!" John stretches across the desk and plants a wet kiss on my mouth. "You're a genius."

I watch as he settles himself in his chair, feet propped on the wall under the mounted screen. As I work, it's hard not to be distracted by his expressions. He's thoroughly engrossed in the movie, and it makes me inexplicably happy.

John laughs at Morris Day's antics, taps his foot to the music, and reacts to every bit of emotion the film elicits. His eyes dance as he watches. He is so fucking beautiful, my heart hurts.

It would be so easy for me to fall in love with this man and knowing that terrifies me. There's so much he keeps hidden from me, I can tell. Too many random texts and phone calls that he claims are Lexi-related. Still, I have no reason to doubt him. And I'm stupid for him.

As a result, my set is subdued, and I program a lot of the tracks, rather than pull vinyl. I can't keep my eyes off John, and I'm worried that I'll scratch a record or miss a cue.

By the time the film ends, and John turns his whiskey eyes on me, I'm... I'm all shaky and weird. I don't understand, I never get like this. Never. Not even with Garrett. I was never this affected, this turned on. This bloody breathless all the bloody time. I don't know myself like this, and I don't know what to do with it. I'm not even sure I like it.

I look away, unable to handle the intensity of John's gaze, and stare unseeing at the computer screen.

John stands and comes around the desk.

"Frankie?"

"Yeah?" I reply without looking up at him. I'm very, very busy, you know.

John drops to one knee and grabs the seat of my chair, spinning me to face him.

"What's up?" I say, trying to control my breathing.

"You okay?" He cards a hand through my hair, cupping my nape with strong fingers. "You seem spooked."

"I..." I shake my head, trying to laugh off this, whatever it is. I feel like I'm coming apart at the seams. Like, if he kisses me or says anything at all to me, I'll lose myself in this. In John.

I'm bloody terrified.

My paltry relationship history hasn't prepared me for this. I'm not ready.

"I'm not ready," I whisper, echoing my thoughts.

"For what?" John flattens his other hand on my thigh, just rests it there, but the touch is soothing.

"I like you too much, I think."

John's smile is slow, sweet, and trembles at the edges. "I feel the same, Nightingale."

I meet his eyes, my lashes fluttering. "Nightingale?"

He's blushing. "It's what I call you in my head, sometimes."

I fucking swoon. Christ, who am I right now? This isn't me.

John cups my face in his hands, his thumbs scrubbing lightly over my stubble. He searches my eyes. It takes everything in me not to look away.

"I know you're worried about moving too fast for me, but are we moving too fast for you?" He asks. "You and Garrett... It hasn't been that long."

I shake my head, effectively cutting him off.

"It isn't Garrett," I confess. "It's... Things don't work like this. They're never this easy."

John gives me a knowing smile. "Let's not borrow trouble," he says before pressing a tender kiss to my lips.

My tongue darts out to taste him before I can even stop myself, and I groan when he pulls back. I press my hands over his, sliding my fingers through his on my cheeks.

"We're figuring this out together, right?"

I nod. "Right, but... You... No more secrets, right?"

John nods, his smile faltering only a little. "What you see is what you get. And it's been good between us, so far. Yeah?" He leans in, nuzzling my nose with his. His words are calm, but I can hear the stutter in his breathing. I can feel his pulse ticking away under my fingertips.

I nod. "Really good. So very good."

John groans at my reply and seals his mouth over mine, sliding his hands behind my head to angle it, putting me where he wants me.

I close my eyes, frowning. Fighting. I don't want to fall this fast, but I don't know how to stop the slide. When I slip my tongue into the wet heat of John's mouth, we both groan on an exhale. The kiss becomes rough and devouring, almost desperate. Hands grabbing, pulses tripping over themselves.

I whimper, and John peppers my lips and cheeks with soft kisses before he eases back to sit on his heels.

"I almost didn't take this job," he says, his voice rough with arousal. "I had another offer, but I thought it would be cool to work in a place like this. Around the music."

"I'm so glad you did," I admit, still shaky.

John's smile is one of relief. I think I'm scaring him.

"I'm glad you're glad, Nightingale, because I can't imagine not knowing you. No matter what," he says, grabbing my hand and squeezing it. "No matter how this turns out, I want to know you. I want you in my life."

His phone pings. John gives my leg one last squeeze before he stands and fishes it out of his pocket. He turns away from me to address whoever it is, and I try not to feel shut out.

John's words should make me feel better, but they don't. I swallow the fear that wants to crawl up out of my throat because the thought of not having John Burton in my life is unfathomable.

I want him. Worse, I think I...

Fuck me, I think I need him.

7

It's hard not to laugh as John climbs into the passenger seat of my Gremlin. I can't help it, he's fucking hilarious. It's like that scene on The Simpsons with the tall man driving the compact car. Like watching a giraffe try to fold himself into a cardboard box.

"I'm glad you're amused," he says as he finally wedges himself into the seat beside me. There's no heat in his voice, so I grin at him.

"We should take your car."

It's Saturday again, and I've invited John to go with me to a giant record fair in Cherry Hill, New Jersey.

He's driven down to my place and found a coveted parking spot on my street that he doesn't want to give up. Parking is at a premium in my neighborhood, and I can see his point, but he looks so uncomfortable.

"I'll be fine." He winces when he bangs his temple on the chicken grip.

"Johnny." I take my key out of the ignition.

He sighs with defeat and turns his head to me.

"Yeah, okay," he finally agrees. "I think I'm beginning to lose feeling in my extremities."

I don't stifle my laughter this time, and John grins begrudgingly.

"Hang on," I tell him as he starts to unspool himself. "Let me come help you."

I get out and jog around the car to grab his hands.

"On one...two...three." I pull, and John pops out of the car like a Jack-in-the-Box.

I catch him in my arms, taking his weight so that he doesn't face-plant in the middle of the street.

John laughs and grabs me tight, planting a kiss on my smiling lips.

"Fucking faggots!"

Gasping, I freeze.

John does too, going rigid in my embrace before he straightens and scrambles away from me.

I turn to see who's uttered the filthy slur. There's no one on the sidewalks or in the street, but a beat-up, black Camaro has just passed us and is turning right at the corner. I draw in a breath to yell at the cowards, but John grabs my shoulder.

"Don't do anything stupid." His voice is strained, small.

With concern brushing aside my rage, I look at him. "It's just some idiot assholes. Don't let it get to you."

His eyes are wide with fear, and his face has gone a shade of pale I've never seen. He quickly puts more distance between us. It stings, but I sort of understand it. John's eyes nervously follow the car until it disappears out of sight.

"Come on." I lock up my car and coax him toward his SUV. "Let's go have some fun."

It only takes us thirty minutes to get to Cherry Hill. The ride is smooth, especially in John's newish Toyota Rav 4, but it's an uncomfortable trip, the lingering stench of the asshole homophobe sits in the air between us.

And the lack of music makes it almost unbearable. If it weren't for the constant soundtrack running in my head, I might not have made it with my sanity intact.

Rage Against the Machine

Rodrick

Rihza

I'm stuck in the Rs.

It isn't until John pulls into a parking space, and turns off the car, that he says anything to me.

"That happen often?" His voice is tight, a grumble.

I don't need to ask what he means.

"Not often, no," I respond honestly. "I can't say it never happens, but it's rare in the city. Even more unusual up in New Bromley. I don't know if you've noticed, but that town is an oasis. I think that's why the station does so well there."

John nods, mulling this over. "Has anyone ever...confronted you? Violently, I mean?" He still isn't looking at me.

I slide a hand onto his thigh and squeeze. "No, Johnny, no one."

He exhales a slow breath and nods sharply. "Good. That's good."

John's hands are still on the steering wheel, his knuckles a little less white now, and he drops one to his lap to take mine. His grip is tight, almost painful, and there's a tick in his jaw.

"Is that something that worries you?" I ask, trying to squeeze his hand. Mine is practically immobilized inside his grasp. "Is that what's kept you from...exploring this side of yourself until now?"

John swallows hard. "I'd really like to say no, but it is part of it." He turns his head to look at me, and I can see how spooked he still is. "Not that I'm worried about getting hurt, I can take care of myself."

"No one would dare attack a bear," I joke, trying to ease the tension in the car.

He huffs out a laugh, but it isn't one of amusement. "You would think."

"Did something happen? In your past?"

John stares ahead. "Is that our turn-off?"

It is, and he maneuvers the car into a parking spot. The lot is crowded, but we get lucky with a spot close to the entrance. I'm distracted from the conversation by the promise of rows and rows and *rows* of records, CDs, and memorabilia that awaits us.

My wallet is burning a hole in my pocket. I turn back to see John taking in the scene, though a shadow still lingers in his expression.

"Come on," I say, scooting closer to place a kiss on his cheek. "Help me find some new music. Music makes everything better." I brush my lips against the corner of his mouth.

John's grip on my hand loosens, and I see a hint of a smile on his plump lips. He bends his head to kiss me full on the mouth, and I melt. As always.

"Are you, uh, looking for anything special today?" He's searching my eyes, asking me about music, but his mind is still clearly elsewhere. Part of me wants to ask, but I let it go.

"Whatever catches my fancy. There is one double ten-inch I've been after for bloody ages, a rare pressing of The Police's *Regatta de Blanc*."

John gives me a blank look.

"It's the album with *Message in a Bottle*, surely you know it."

His face brightens. "Yeah, I do. I didn't know that was the same band that did *Roxanne*."

I. Am. Incredulous. "Really?"

Pffft. As if Sting's voice isn't distinctive.

I open my door and climb out into the bright sunshine. It's a damned beautiful, autumn day, and I'm anxious to shake off the negative vibes and spend some time with my guy and my music.

My guy.

Bloody hell.

I'm grinning by the time John comes around the car to me.

One corner of his mouth lifts in a smile. "What's so funny?"

"Nothing," I say, stretching up to kiss him.

Before I can connect, John pulls back and glances around, shoving his hands into his pockets.

I have to remind myself that we just had an ugly moment. While I'm able to brush off shit like that, most of the time, John's still new to this. It's only natural for him to be gun shy. Right?

Still, I can't say I'm not disappointed that we won't be strolling hand-in-hand through the fair. John isn't ready for that. Not now, anyway. And, as my dear Gran used to say, I have "the patience of Job."

An hour after we arrive, I'm haggling with a vendor over a rare Kelis pressing when John gets a call and excuses himself. I wait for him for a full fifteen minutes before I get nervous and go looking.

I exhale with relief when I find him, though his features are pinched once again. He offers up a tight smile.

"Everything okay?"

He nods, short and sharp. "Just a call from Lexi's grandmother."

"Oh." I squeeze his bicep. The muscle tenses under my palm, and I drop my arm to my side, sighing inwardly. "Let's go get some funnel cake."

John's smile warms a little. "I love funnel cake."

Glad to pull him out of whatever funk the phone call has created, I grin up at him. "Who doesn't?"

***

"Why did you and Garrett split?"

We've just polished off three cartons of Thai food, and I'm nearly in a food coma. Being with John might be dangerous for my waistline.

I'm flipping through the two crates of vinyl I'd scored at the fair and almost miss the question, utterly enamored with my findings. Vintage Nine Inch Nails, a copy of Nirvana's *Nevermind* - still in the fucking plastic! - and a bit of colored vinyl from a band I've never heard of, which is excellent for decoration unless I uncover a hidden gem. That's happened on a few occasions.

"Hmm?" I turn my head to look at him. John is eyeing me with keen interest, but I wonder what's brought this up.

"Too personal?"

I shake my head. I'd almost forgotten his question. "No, of course not."

"You don't talk much about him."

John picks up the copy of *The Downward Spiral* I'd grabbed for five bucks. An absolute steal!

"I'm curious. Of course, I'm curious. But we don't need to talk about it if it makes you uncomfortable."

"It doesn't make me uncomfortable." It doesn't. Maybe it should, I don't know. "To be honest, I don't think about Garrett much these days."

John gives me a pointed look. "No?"

"Well," I say, stretching my leg out until my toes reach his thigh. "My thoughts have been otherwise occupied, haven't they?"

He gives me a small grin, but it falls quickly. "What's he like?"

I think about Garrett, his larger-than-life personality, his confidence that the world owed him nothing but its best. I think about the way he was with me, alternately attentive and dismissive.

"He's a good guy. Solid. Reliable."

John narrows his eyes. "Sounds more like your insurance agent than your ex."

I snort. "He'd wither to hear you say that. No, Garrett is all of those things. He's probably the most self-assured person I know. The most comfortable in his own skin. With his place in the world."

"More than Dyer?"

"Dyer's confidence is performative, a lot of it."

John frowns. "Really? If you'd asked me, I'd say *he's* the most confident person I'd ever met."

"Not me?"

He lifts his brows. "You? No. You're…"

I expect him to say any number of things. That I'm neurotic, high-maintenance, under-achieving, aloof.

"You're present."

It's my turn to frown. "Present?"

His eyes search the ceiling for a moment, hopefully looking for a better way to explain. "You're here and now. You don't live in the past, you're not overly concerned with the future. You're in the present."

I blink. He's not wrong. "Is that good or bad?"

"It's just how you are," John replies.

My hands drop to my lap, though I'm careful not to damage the sleeve of the record I'm holding. I'm not a navel-gazer by nature, but John's words have me thinking.

"Garrett and I burned at different temperatures," I say. It feels odd to perform an autopsy on my failed relationship with my new boyfriend. "We had very different ideas about what being in a relationship meant."

"Did he sleep around?"

"If he did, I wasn't aware of it," I admit. "I don't think so, no. But he had so many limits. So many rules."

John shifts around to lean his back against the sofa, next to me.

"Our friends were his friends. Our schedule was essentially his schedule. He took care of practically everything. Not because I'm incapable, but because he preferred it that way. Liked being in control." The more I talk, the more I remember the resentment I felt towards Garrett, especially at the end.

"I honestly can't imagine you living by someone else's rules, not if they didn't line up with your own."

I smile. "You would think that, but I..., I tend to just go along with whatever."

"Really?"

"It makes things easy." I shrug. "I hate conflict."

John seems genuinely surprised. "I've never met anyone as self-possessed as you."

"Mate, you need to get out more." I grin at him. "But, really, I tend to go along with whatever. I'm easy, except..."

"Except with this." John gestures around us at the vinyl scattered on the floor. "And with your work."

I nod. "Yeah."

"You're very easy to get along with. Easy to talk to," John says, and my face heats up.

"I've ever been good at compliments," I say when he smiles at my blush.

"I'm not really trying to compliment you, just stating facts."

"Thanks anyway."

"I say that because I do wonder what it was that came between you and Garrett. Really."

"I told you, he hates this." I sweep my arm over the records and sleeves, the notes, and old magazines. "Couldn't stand my...obsession, he called it."

"But we just established that no one is going to change this about you," he said. John runs a hand through his hair. "I don't know why anyone would *want* to. Your relationship with music is a gift."

Okay, I think I could love this man.

"So, I get the feeling it's something else."

"You really want to know?"

John nods slowly. "I really want to know."

"Garrett has a shaky relationship with openness." I flick my eyebrows in acknowledgment of John's confusion. "Yeah, it's weird for a guy who is so outspoken about everything from politics to wine to the length of my fingernails. Don't ask," I say preemptively.

"I don't think I want to know."

"You don't," I agree. "Anyway, Garrett was deceptively open, except about the things that mattered. He didn't trust me with the big stuff. Like, when his parents announced they were getting divorced. I didn't hear the news from G, I heard it over dinner at one of his friend's houses."

"Damn."

"Everyone at the table knew except for me, his boyfriend. The guy he was practically living with." I can feel myself getting riled up. I stop to take a deep breath.

"Sorry," John says, his voice tender.

I shake my head. "It's okay. It's just... Like you said, I can go with the flow or whatever, no problem, but I hate being shut out. When I'm with someone, I want to share the good and the bad. Not just the Hallmark moments."

John straightens up, and his lips press into a thin line. I don't know what to make of this shift in his mood. Maybe he wants to ask me more about Garrett and me. I'll tell him whatever he wants to know, but I don't want to talk about my ex. We're over. Completely.

I reach over and palm John's thigh. "I don't think about the past much. What's done is done. And the future scares me, to be honest. I mean, look at the state of the world. I try not to think about where I'll be beyond next week. Next month. Garrett has a bloody five-ten-fifteen plan." I roll my eyes.

He slides his hand over mine and gives my fingers a squeeze. "I'm sorry I brought it up."

"Don't be," I assure him and muster up a smile. "I'm with you. I'm here with you, right now, and I'm...happy."

His eyes light up. "Yeah?"

I smile because how could he not know that? "Yes, pet. Very. You?"

John bites his lip, something I haven't seen him do before. Not due to him being nervous, which he clearly is. Under half-lidded eyes and around a sexy growl? Oh, all the time. Mmmm.

"Why don't you stay at my place this weekend?"

"Huh?" I'm probably gaping like a fish, but he's caught me off-guard.

"You haven't been over yet," he rushes to say and takes my hand in his, almost sheepish. "Come spend the rest of the weekend with me. We could go somewhere new for brunch tomorrow, and you'd be closer to work on Monday when your shift comes around. We could spend the day together."

"You don't have work on Monday?"

John drops my hand and reaches for the takeaway carton of Pad Thai that's probably cold by now. He's covering for his nerves. It's adorable.

"School's out Monday and Tuesday, and I don't have any jobs lined up. So, no." He plucks an errant noodle out of one of the cardboard boxes and slurps it down.

Have I mentioned how much I love to watch John eat?

Erotic visions aside, this is a big step for us, and Dyer's questions slip right into my mind.

Though John and I spend a lot of time together, we've yet to spend a whole night. I've been careful not to push him into something before he's ready. Other than a couple of handjobs, and several dozen epic make-out sessions, our relationship has been rather chaste. Swoon-worthy, but chaste. The thing is, though I want more,

I'm happy with us as-is. I wonder if he's feeling pressured, though. Have I pressured him?

John must sense my hesitation.

"No expectations," he says, cupping the back of my neck. "I have a spare room if that makes you feel more comfortable. I just... I want to spend more time with you."

My heart does a somersault in my chest. "Yeah?"

"Uh, yeah." He says this like I'm thick. "Why does that surprise you?"

"It doesn't," I say quickly.

John inches closer, leaving no space between us, and we're pressed together from hip to thigh.

I've only turned on two of the lamps in my living room, and the walls merely glow softly around us. I'd thrown on some Lamb and Portishead for dinner. The atmosphere is very romantic if I do say so myself.

"I think you underestimate my level of interest." John's hand, which he's lifted to sift through the hair at my nape, drifts down to cup the back of my neck. He leans in and brushes his nose across my late-day stubble.

I can hear the scritch-scritch of his skin as it skims over the coarse hairs. It's a steady rhythm, and I feel my heartbeat slowing to match it.

"You think so?" My voice wavers a little, which makes him lean back and smile. He has to know what he does to me.

John nods and leans in close, brushing his nose against mine now. It seems to be a favorite thing for him to do.

My eyelids flutter shut. Jesus, this man. He's such a sweetheart, so tender and gentle, and yet so powerful. It's a dangerous combination.

"Come home with me." His voice pours over me like melted chocolate.

I sag against him, dropping my forehead to his shoulder.

His hand slides across my shoulders and he starts to massage. I didn't realize I was so tense.

"What're you afraid of?"

I shake my head, and he slides his fingers up into my unruly mop of curls.

"I'm terrified of pushing you too fast," I confess into the soft wool of his sweater. "I'm hyper-aware that I'm your first... Like this."

John cards his hand through my hair, his fingertips dancing along my scalp. He's very tactile, which I love. I hate to compare, but it's hard not to. Garrett was never this demonstrative, this attentive. This open. If he had been, I might still be with him. This attention is damned addictive.

"Are you a serial killer?"

His fingers still at my question. "What?"

I huff out a laugh. "You have to have some skeletons in your closet."

John's fingers resume their heavenly press against my skull, but his voice sounds different. "Why do you say that?"

"Because you're too bloody perfect," I whine. "You're gorgeous, successful, grounded..."

"You think I'm gorgeous?" I don't need to look at him to know he's smiling.

I slide my hand up along his muscular thigh, squeezing gently. Loving the feel of him.

"You know you are," I retort.

"I really don't," he replies, and I sit up to look at him.

He's serious.

"You're serious."

He shrugs. "To be honest, it's not something I ever think about, but if you think so, then I'm glad." John brushes a thumb across my lips. "Anything that can hold your interest, I'll take. Maybe I need to start hitting the gym."

"Please, no," I gasp, clutching one of his forearms. They're fucking huge. "If you get any hotter, I'll get a complex."

John grins at me, his eyes riveted to my mouth. "A complex?"

"I already think I'm not good enough for you," I confess, surprised by the truth of it.

John frowns. "You..." He frames my face in his hands. I'm forced to meet his eyes, and they shine with sincerity. "You're more than I could have ever hoped for."

God.

I stare, blinking drunkenly into his bourbon-soaked gaze.

"Yes," I answer, finally, and he looks confused. "Let's go to your place."

8

I don't know what I was expecting from the residence of a man as talented with his hands as John is, but this isn't it.

He lives in a cinderblock monstrosity off industrial route 202. And while the flat is a good size, with two generous bedrooms plus a small den, a full kitchen, and a living room big enough to entertain more than a handful of friends, it's...in a word...rubbish.

"It's nice," I say because what he's done with it is homey, in a way. There are little touches here and there that warm up the otherwise cold space.

There's barely any natural light, so John has off-white, rice-paper lanterns scattered in the corners. He flips them on, all eight of them, with one switch. The effect is lovely.

But where my parlor is a riot of colors and textures, wood grain furniture, hardwood floors, and various rugs of unknown origin, John's is nearly industrial.

Thin carpet, the color of almond milk, flows from wall to wall in every room but the kitchen and bathroom. The walls are a similar shade of baby vomit, with nothing to hide the building's cinderblock roots. The texture of the walls reminds me of the one night I spent in jail for a drunk and disorderly.

This place is depressing as fuck. No wonder John always makes the drive down to the city to see me.

"You're being kind, and I appreciate it, but I hate it here."

John's expression must mimic mine because his dislike for the flat is written all over his beautiful face.

"It's not that bad," I swear. "I love what you've done with it."

"The only room I can stand to be in, really, is my bedroom."

"Well now," I say, walking up to him and sliding my arms around his waist. "Of course, it is." I wiggle my eyebrows, just to let him know I'm teasing.

We've already established that there are no expectations for this slumber party. But yeah, I'm pretty sure we're going to end up naked.

John's arm comes around my waist, and his other hand goes to my hip. Squeezing. Pulling me into his body. He drops his head to my shoulder as the hand on my hips slides down over my ass. He gives one cheek a hard squeeze.

It's such a promise, that one small thing.

I feel him take a deep breath, and then he sighs sweetly. I melt even further into his embrace.

"You always smell so good," he says into my neck. "Like amber and vanilla and...juniper or something?"

"It's just a combination of products," I reply, shivering because his hand has moved up under my sweater to stroke at the small of my back. My skin there is on fire.

I never knew I was so sensitive.

After pressing a loud, wet kiss on the side of my neck that has me hardening immediately, he lets me go. I groan as his hands slide from my body.

I want them back. Right now.

"Something to drink?" He saunters into the kitchen.

As much as I hate that he's walking away from me, I enjoy the view as he leaves. I'm so busy watching his arse as he moves, remembering the feel of it in my hands and plotting how I can get to it again, I almost forget to answer.

"Sure. Uh, whatever's cold."

"Iron Ale okay?" He calls from the other room.

"Perfect," I reply, taking in more of his decor.

The porridge-colored, fiberboard, Ikea cube leaning against the wall, six squares by six squares, is filled with books. There are also photos of his family, I presume, and small stacks of CDs, old receipts, and other random bits on the twelve-inch shelves. It has a look of contained chaos about it, which actually personalizes the space nicely. Well, at least the one wall.

I step closer to inspect the photographs. There's one with John and who I assume are his parents. It looks like a graduation picture, and John's baby face makes me smile. His dimple is just so adorable.

Another pic shows John with two girls. They have the same whiskey-colored eyes and the same easy smile. His sisters, I'm guessing. It seems to have been taken at least a decade ago.

There's a photo of John with a bunch of teenagers in front of what looks like a classroom. At the bottom of the picture, it says Walt Whitman High School, Edgerton, Pennsylvania.

Huh.

I file that bit of information away for later.

"Here you go."

John's step falters as he approached, his gaze darting from mine to the photos on the shelves.

I plaster on a smile and move away from them as he hands me a pint glass filled with a golden liquid. We clink, and I take a sip.

"It's good," I say, fascinated by the workings of his throat as he swallows.

John nods. "Isn't it? I had a client up from the city. We went to Rick's Pub, the new place that replaced the BC Inn, off Main. They had this on tap, and I bought a growler."

"I've been meaning to go there. Is the food any good?"

"Yeah, it's not bad, actually. And I met the owner, Rick." John takes my hand and leads me to the sectional that takes up most of the living room's floor space. It also sits under the room's only window. "Nice guy, amiable. And so knowledgeable. The way you are with music, that's how he is with beer. You'll like him. We'll go soon."

I arch an eyebrow. "You obviously like him."

John's smile is wicked. "Is that a hint of jealousy I see?"

"Pffft." I scoff and take another sip from the beer, which is delicious. "It was an observation."

"Well, he is very attractive."

"Yeah?"

"Ohhh, yeah," he says, gazing up at the ceiling with a dreamy expression. "Tall, broad, with golden skin, thick black hair, and a great smile."

John crosses his leg and rests his ankle on his knee, the very picture of innocence, but I can see the red creeping up his neck.

I smack him on his bicep, just as he brings his glass to his lips.

"Ooof!" He sputters and coughs, wiping his chin with his hand and trying not to laugh. "Careful."

"Stop trying to wind me up," I warn, smirking at him.

"You should know by now I only have eyes for one person."

John sets his glass down and takes mine from my hand.

"Hey, I'm not done with..."

His lips are cold, but his mouth is warm and yeasty. There's a bite of hops on his tongue when it wraps around mine, but beneath it all, it's just John.

I savor him, losing myself in the kiss almost instantly, and my cock stirring from its not-so-restful slumber.

John's hands are all over me. I've never seen him like this before, so needy and insistent. He's usually so reserved, so tentative. Never holding me too tightly, or kissing me too long. I like him like this, so close to the edge so soon.

I run my hands over him, over the cotton of his shirt to feel the hard planes of his muscles. He's so big and so solid, I can't help but feel safe with him. Protected. I've never needed to feel protected before, had never wanted to be. But with John, I want the circle of his strong arms around me. I crave it. I fear I might die without it.

His fingers tweak one of my nipples, and I moan into yet another kiss. John nibbles down my throat and around to my ear. He's panting hard, but so am I.

"I...I know we said slow, but..."

"I want you too, John." I clutch him to me, unable to get enough of him around me. "Just tell me what you want."

He leans back to meet my eyes. His are dark, darker than I've ever seen them, the pupils completely blown.

His mouth is claret red, his cheeks flushed.

God.

He's dazzling.

"Come to my bed, Nightingale," he husks, and my dick jerks in my jeans.

And yet, a note of warning sounds in my head. "John..."

"Slow is still on the agenda, I just..." He exhales harshly and runs a rough hand through his hair. "I want to feel you, all of you against me with nothing between us. Skin to skin." He searches my eyes, his fingers ghosting over my swollen lips.

I suck the tip of his index finger into my mouth and run my tongue over it.

The groan he gives me is throaty and needy and, fuck, so damned sexy.

"I need this. You, Frankie. I need you."

I nod, mesmerized by the want I see in him. "I need you too."

John was right. His bedroom is the best room in his flat. It's cozy and inviting, with a king-sized sleigh bed against one wall, a leather armchair in the corner by a balcony door, an armoire so large it nearly touches the eight-foot ceiling, and a mirrored dresser.

Off to the right, there's a door leading to what I presume is a bathroom. Another set of doors opposite seems to lead to a closet.

I have about fifteen seconds to take it all in before John's hot mouth is back on mine, insistent and greedy. His hands frame my face, which I love, love, love.

This feeling of being possessed, treasured, I've never had it. Never knew what I was missing until now. Until John Burton.

"May I?" John breaks the kiss and tugs at the hem of my long-sleeved Reverend Horton Heat tee.

I lift my arms, expecting him to whip it off, but he goes slowly.

Peeling it over my up-stretched limbs like he's unwrapping a gift. It isn't like he's never seen me shirtless before, he has. Multiple times. But he's looking at me like it's the first time.

That look has me trembling. I can only stand here, mute. My skin prickling with the need to have him touch me again.

"And you?" His voice hovers just about a whisper. "What do you want, Franklin?"

"Please," I hear myself say. "Please, just... Touch me."

John's hands shake as he reaches for my belt buckle, but he quickly does away with it, and soon my jeans are sliding down my legs. He follows them down to the floor and helps me step out of, first my beat-up Vans, and then the worn denim.

When he stands again, he runs the tip of his index finger inside the waistband of my boxer-briefs. His fingernail scrapes over my abdomen and, I swear to all that is holy, I think I'm going to come just from that.

John's eyes zero in on my erection, where it peeks out of the top of the elastic band, his expression that of a starving man.

In one fluid movement, he strips me of the cotton briefs, pushing them down over my hips. I let them drop, step out of them, and suddenly I'm naked, my cock slapping against my belly.

I've never felt more exposed.

It's a first for us, well, for me.

He's still dressed.

"This is so not fair." I curse the tremor in my voice.

Wordlessly, John raises his arms, and I lift his jumper over his head and toss in on the pile with my clothing. Next to go is his t-shirt, and I move right along to the button on his jeans. I need to see him. Feel him.

"I sort of envy that you don't need a belt to hold these up," I whisper.

"Why?" His smile trembles at the corners, and I can see his pulse hammering away at the base of his throat.

I have the overwhelming urge to kiss him there, and so I do. "It's your incredible thighs," I whisper into the hollow.

"I-is it?" He shudders when I run my tongue over his Adam's apple.

"Yeah," I husk, My erection, bobbing helplessly between us, is steadily dripping precome. "And your glorious fucking arse."

"Ohh, *arse*," he says, poking fun at my accent, which tends to come out when I'm excited. Or aroused. Or nervous.

At the moment, I'm all three.

"Yes," I say against his hard, right pec, my fingers deftly opening his jeans and pushing them down. I follow them, licking streaks down his skin as I go. Kissing. Biting gently.

His breath catches.

John toes out of his Skechers and lifts, first one leg, then the other as I strip him of his jeans.

His eyes are hot on my face as I slide the last remaining piece of clothing between us down his legs, and he kicks it off. I'm dimly aware of them landing in a corner somewhere.

Now we're standing naked, staring into one another's eyes. When I glance down, I see our cocks bobbing in tandem, stiff. Dancing, like they're ready to duel.

John steps closer, and I shiver when I feel his erection brush against mine. He tilts his head and kisses me hot and brief, then steps back - way back - and looks at me.

He just...looks at me. His gaze travels from my head of damp curls down to my nipples, which pebble from his gaze, and finally down to my cock. It lingers there a moment or three before returning to my eyes.

I've never been self-conscious about my body. I know my plusses and minuses, but I squirm under his gaze.

"Fucking hell, Nightingale," John breathes. "You're so goddamned beautiful."

Heat flushes over every inch of my skin as he takes two quick steps and claims my mouth, one hand behind my neck, one on my hip, before walking me backward and lowering me down to the bed.

The duvet is soft against my back, the cotton cool against my overheated skin. And John is hard. Everywhere. And hot, scorching hot, all over me.

I reach between us and wrap my fingers around his erection, and it pulses in my hand.

John hisses and buries his hands in my hair. He turns my head the way he wants it so that he can plunder my mouth, and I take it all. Everything he wants to give me, I want it. Desperately.

He sucks on my tongue, hard, as he pumps into my fist, and I moan like a porn star. My dick slides along the smooth planes of his abdomen, leaving wet streaks of need on his golden skin.

John devours me, licking the roof of my mouth, the inside of my cheeks, leaving no part unexplored.

I give as good as I get, writhing underneath him. Wrapping my legs around his waist and holding on for dear life. My arm around his neck is like a vise, I know, but I can't control it. I want him too much, and I'm afraid of the wanting.

"What do you want, John?" I pant the words into his neck when we come up for air. I pump him in time with my panting breaths.

"If you keep touching me like that, I'm going to come."

I still my hand, but don't release him. "Not yet."

"No, not yet. I want inside you," he practically begs. "But I don't think we should start with that."

"Where do you want to start, love? Tell me." I can barely breathe.

"I want to kiss you everywhere," he husks.

And yes, please. That.

John rolls me to my stomach with an ease that surprises me. Fuck, he's strong.

He runs his roughened hands over the smooth skin of my ass, and I arch, instinctively, into his touch, my hole already fluttering with anticipation.

A light smack on my right butt cheek makes me squeal.

John's hands still on my skin. "What was that noise?"

I don't bloody well know, I've never made it before.

"You startled me," I protest. The spot stings, but not for long. It tingles for a different reason when I feel his lips there, then his tongue, soothing me.

"I've had dreams about this ass," he rumbles, once again smoothing his hands over me.

Sturdy fingers massage my flesh, knead it. My ass, my thighs, the muscles of my back melt under John's ministrations.

Something warm and wet licks up my spine, and I gasp, arching into the hard body now pressed against me.

John's cock is notched in my crease, and I automatically pull my knees up to spread my legs.

"Fuck," he growls. "Babe, don't tempt me. Please."

I pump my hips, grinding into the mattress and letting him slide over my opening. I can feel my greedy, little pucker loosen with anticipation.

John's hand is tight on my hip, and I still, the length of him trapped between my cheeks, his hot breath fanning over my neck and shoulder.

"Jesus," he sighs.

"Take me…"

"No," he snaps, before lifting up off of me.

I can't stop the noise of protest from leaving my throat. John doesn't give me time to complain, I'm suddenly on my back again, looking up at him.

His eyes are wild, his lips dark red and ravaged. Beads of sweat have formed on his forehead, and I want to lick them off. I reach up and slide a hand into his hair, run my other fingers along the dips and curves of his back.

His cock is so thick and covered in a map of veins I hope to memorize with my tongue. It rests on the crease where my hip meets my thigh, right next to my own. Hot and hard and desert dry.

I've never been with a man that didn't dribble when he was aroused.

Me, I'm a bloody faucet, leaking all over my stomach.

"What's this?" He brushes a fingertip over the tattoo to the left of my groin.

It's a musical phrase. Eight notes.

He studies them, frowning like he's trying to work them out.

"Do you read music?"

John shakes his head. "Not really. I remember 'Good Boys Deserve Fudge Always' from elementary school." He grins and looks up at me.

I laugh. "A handy trick." I take John's hand and press his index finger along the line of notes. I hum the line to him and search his face for recognition.

He shakes his head, his eyes locked in mine.

"It's from the Police, a song called *Tea in the Sahara*." I'd gotten the tattoo when I was at university, after a break-up. I think the song is about longing. About waiting for someone to come along and love you. Someone who'll stay.

John nods like he can hear my thoughts, but says "I've never heard it."

"We'll fix that." The words come out on a shuddering breath because John lowers his head to my skin, lips brushing over the ink.

"God," I gasp. "You're driving me crazy."

"I think you should have me first," he says, so softly I almost don't hear him.

I put my hands on his shoulders and push. Honestly, I don't think I could budge him if he didn't want me to, but he rises and lifts his fathomless, bourbon eyes to mine.

"You want... Y-you want me to fuck you?" I need to make sure I'm understanding him because this is not what I thought would happen tonight. John has "top" written all over him, even if he hasn't experimented with either topping or bottoming.

"Yes," he says, searching my eyes. "I'm new to this, yeah?"

I nod, reaching up to hold his face in my hands.

"I want you to have me first so that I can learn what you like, what feels good. I don't want my first time with you to run the risk of my hurting you, babe."

Oh, God.

"John..." It's all I can say. I'm speechless.

He's kissing down my chest to my nipples, where he sucks and laves each one until I'm squirming beneath him.

"I never want to hurt you." John's lips nip at my stomach, my pelvis. He lowers his face to my groin and inhales. "Never."

"I know," I say. And I do. I know it in my bones.

I also know how much he wants me. It's there in the tremble of his hands as they ghost over my thighs. With every touch, he promises to bring me to the pinnacle of pleasure, to lay claim to my body. But the worry that he might hurt me through his inexperience has him almost shaking out of his skin.

I spend one delicious, mind-blowing moment encased in the wet bliss of John's mouth before he pops off and lifts his head to meet my eyes.

God, he looks so damned terrified.

"So, will you?"

"Fuck yeah," I say, smiling down at him.

John barks out a relieved laugh, even as his cock twitches against my shin.

"C'mere," I demand. The relief reaches his eyes, and it makes me smile.

John surges up and kisses me, sweetly at first, but then our mutual hunger kicks back in. Soon we're burning up, devouring each other.

While I ache to have John buried deep inside me, to feel him unleash all of his power upon me, my hunger for him spikes my bloodstream like a new song by a favorite band. The very thought of *me* being inside *him*, the idea of me teaching him this pleasure, makes me dizzy. He needs this from me. Needs me. Maybe we're on even ground now.

I grow impatient. "Do you have stuff?"

"Yeah," he grunts into my neck.

The cold in the room seeps into my skin in the brief time it takes for him to go to his nightstand and return. I pull the covers back and crawl into bed, John hot on my heels. His sheets are soft, jersey cotton, and I stretch against them.

John hands me a tiny bottle of lube and an envelope.

"What's this?" I ask, removing the paper, though I already know.

He bites his lip. "You can read it if you need to, but everything came back negative."

I set the paper aside and look at the bottle of lube. Then I look up at him.

"I already have everything I need."

9

John's watching me intently, something he often does, but right now, it's making me a little nervous. I haven't been with a virgin since I was sixteen. And although John isn't technically a virgin, I can't help but feel like I'm about to deflower him. I grin down at him, stretched out underneath me.

"What?" He says, one corner of his mouth lifting with a fluttering smile.

"I was just thinking, I feel like I'm about to defile you."

His laugh is long and loud, and my nerves ease a bit at the sound of it.

"Be gentle with me," he says in a small voice, batting his thick, feathery eyelashes, and then laughs loudly again.

I smack him on his rock-hard abs.

"Ow," he says.

"Ow!" I say, shaking out my hand. "You're made of bloody granite."

"You like me when I'm hard," he says, laughing.

The laugh turns into a moan when I slide down the bed and take the length of him into my mouth.

"Oh, fuck..."

His murmur of delight turns me on. I moan, and suck, and lick, and nibble, and give John Burton's cock every bit of pleasure I can dream up.

Johnny reaches for me. His fingers curl around the back of my head, urging me up.

"I don't wanna come like that," he pants, grinning. "Not right now, anyway."

"I will drink you down," I tell him because it's something I truly need to do, and soon. But he's right, not this time.

Giving his gorgeous dick one last lick, I climb up his body. The slightest of pulls from his hand on my nape has me leaning down to him, but he stops my descent before I can touch my lips to his.

"You can do anything you want to me, Frankie."

The trust, the belief that I'll do right by him, it floors me.

"I'll make it so good for you."

"I know."

I stretch out beside him, draw his leg up and drape it over mine. John bends his other leg and lets it fall to the side, opening himself to me without my even asking. His eyes lock on mine.

"I won't hurt you," I promise," but it will feel a little strange at first."

He nods.

"Trust me?"

"Yes," he answers without hesitation. His expression is so open, so vulnerable, and it brushes up against a tender spot near my heart. Presses against it like a finger to a bruise.

I smooth my hand up the inside of his thigh to his groin and lower my mouth to his. He returns my hungry kiss as I take his erection and stroke it, running my thumb over the tip, eliciting an appreciative moan from deep in his throat.

His cock feels incredible in my hand. All of him feels amazing against me, hot and hard, and waiting.

After a few strokes, and a kiss that never wants to end, I sit up and grab the bottle of lube from behind me. I squirt a generous amount over my fingers and slick his cock, encouraging him to pump into my hand.

"Frankie," he pants as his hips flex.

His face and neck flush a dark red, and that's when I know he's ready for more.

Using some of the excess lube, I slide my other fingers along his crease.

He tenses but relaxes as I stroke over his taint. I love the feel of him there, hot and a little rough under my fingertips. As his skin heats, his earthy musk hits my senses, making my mouth water.

His heat, his scent, the sounds he's making for me, because of me, they drive me insane. I need to get my mouth back on him.

Perched on one elbow, I position my lips over the swollen head of his cock and lift my eyes to his face. I blow a stream of warm air over the sensitive tip, and his eyes snap shut on a moan.

"Watch me," I command softly.

His eyes open, half-lidded with lust, and I lick my bottom lip, sucking it into my mouth and biting it before I stretch my tongue out to taste him.

Hints of the lube hit my palate first, followed by the salt of his skin and, finally, the essence of him.

I swirl my tongue around the tip, exploring every bump and ridge, every dip and curve.

John groans. "You look so good between my legs," he says, his voice rough with arousal. "So fucking good."

I suck him into my mouth, dipping my head to take as much of him as I can. He's wide and stretches my lips almost to the point of discomfort, but I am too hungry to care. I can feel the tremor in his hips as he struggles not to thrust up into my mouth. When I run a slick fingertip around his hole, he loses the battle, surging up and into the back of my throat.

We both moan.

"Fuck," he hisses.

"Mmmm," I respond, humming around his length.

I experiment, pushing the blunt tip of my finger against his puckered ring. The lube allows me in, just a bit, and John gasps.

I let him slide out of my mouth.

"You okay?"

He nods frantically, his head on the pillow. "Yeah...yes. It's...yeah."

"Weird?"

He lets out a soft, shaky laugh. "Yeah, a little."

"Do you want me to stop, or do you want more?" I'm pressing in, even as I ask the question. His hole flexes around my fingertip, suckles at it.

"M-more," he breathes.

I use another finger to push more lube toward his opening and push in. I'm up to my knuckle in his tight heat. My own cock jumps and dribbles against my thigh as I imagine being buried inside him.

"You are so tight, Johnny," I whisper. "I can't wait to be inside you."

"Oh, God, I want you there."

"Do you?" I ask, slipping a second finger inside his gorgeous ass.

John widens his legs, his thighs shaking uncontrollably.

"Yes," he sighs. "Yes. Fuck, I need..."

"I know."

I take him into my mouth and twist my fingers inside him, searching for the spot I know will drive him out of his head. When I find it, John's hips fly off the bed. I nearly choke on the thickness now shoved down my throat.

I swallow and breathe through my nose while I stroke over his prostate.

John's ass hits the mattress, but I follow him down, fucking him with my mouth as I mercilessly stroke his sweet spot.

"Fuck...shit...Frankie...shit, what the...fuck?" He's panting, gulping down air like he's afraid it will all disappear.

I release him from my mouth and grin up at him.

His eyes are hot, heavy-lidded, and focused on me.

"Haven't you ever explored?" I'm pumping my fingers into him now, ready to add a third.

"I...no. I mean, I've touched my, uh, hole, but I've never...I mean, I didn't..."

"You never searched for your prostate?"

He shakes his head.

"Oh, baby," I croon, adding another finger. I screw them into him, stretching him gently, opening him up. The glide is smooth. He's nearly ready for me. "I'm gonna make you feel so good, you'll think you're flying."

John shudders, his breath ghosting out of him. He presses his head back into the pillow.

"I'm not sure how much more I can take," he laughs.

I slide my fingers free, thrilled to feel that his body is reluctant to let me go. Grabbing the bottle of lube, I dribble a generous amount down his taint. After closing the cap and tossing the lube out of the way, I work the wetness into his opening with my thumb.

"Frankie," John moans. "I need more."

"I know, love." I lift my head to meet his eyes. "I'm here."

Kneeling between his spread legs, I take in the sight of him.

John's lean, sculpted body laid out beneath me is like something out of a dream. He's easily the most beautiful man I've ever had in my bed. But it's more than his physical beauty, there's...a connection between us that I can't explain.

Even now, with his eyes locked on mine, there's a silent conversation taking place.

I grab my cock, sheathing and slicking it up before I guide the tip to his quivering hole.

Slowly, gently, I push forward.

John's breath catches as I easily breach the ring of muscle at his entrance.

I pause, giving him time to get used to me. And giving myself time to regain some control. The feel of him, tight around me, is almost too much to bear.

"Keep going," he says, his voice low.

I move my hips forward, inching into his channel. Fuck, he's scorching hot around my dick. I shake my head.

"It's so much," I mutter.

"More," he responds.

John is handling this much better than I am. I'm about to lose all of my molecules, about to become stardust.

He hooks his legs over my hips, angling his pelvis up, and suddenly I'm all the way inside him. We both cry out, the searing heat of him clutching my cock, it's...fuck, it's...

John thrusts his hips up, his hands fisting the sheet beneath him.

I take the hint and start to move. The glide is smooth, perfect. And so damned tight, I start to babble.

"I'm fucking you, Johnny," I say, the words tumbling out of my mouth. "Do you feel me? Feel that? I'm inside you. You're all around me, so hot and so tight and so bloody perfect. Fuck! John..."

He reaches up and pulls me down, his arms circling my back.

My mouth falls over his, the kiss a wild imitation of what we're doing. My cock, buried in his ass, pistons in and out in steady strokes.

His tongue explores every part of my mouth. His hands roam over my skin, clutching, claiming. One slides up my neck and into my hair, where he grabs a fistful of my curls, pulling me down into his hungry, greedy kiss.

John's hips set the rhythm. All I can do is hold on for the ride, no longer in control. He grunts and groans with every stroke.

I change the angle of my hips so that my cock pegs his gland with each thrust, and John's mouth leaves mine.

He screams, his voice hoarse, and I nearly come just from the sound of it. My brain latches onto the rhythm of us, me driving into him. It's primal, a timeless, innate coming together of bodies. Push. Pull. Push. Pull.

Nine Inch Nails fills my head. I'm fucking Johnny like an animal, getting closer to God, using the rhythm of the music to drive us both insane.

John begins to chant. "Frankie, Frankie, Frankie...fuck. Fuck! I'm gonna..."

I lift up, supporting my weight on one arm as I grab his cock and stroke him, My pace brutal as I slam into him over and over.

John is cursing, babbling, clawing at me. I know he'll leave marks on my skin. I want him to. I want him to brand me. It's a need I didn't even know I had.

Two more pumps of my fist and John comes. Thick, ropey strands land on his abdomen, my stomach, my fist, his chest. A bit lands on his chin, and I lower my head to lick it off.

John's muscles flex and clench all around me. Between that exquisite pressure, and the taste of him, and I can't hold on anymore.

I drop my head to John's chest, coming so hard the edges of my vision blur. I feel the flood of warmth and wet surround my cock as I pulse, spilling into the condom.

John murmurs nonsense into my skin, holding me so tightly I can barely breathe.

Suddenly, oxygen is at a premium.

"John," I croak, and he eases his grip.

"Sorry." He smoothes his hands over my back.

I rest atop him, his heart pound against my chest and my own answering in kind. Between us, our skin is slick and sticky, but I can't be arsed to care.

Our mingled scents fill the air, and I breathe in deep. I can't move, don't want to, and John seems content to have me covering him.

He kisses my neck, my shoulder, runs his fingers through my sweaty hair.

I feel my softening dick slip from his body, and a wave of sadness comes over me. I take care of the condom, and then wind my arms tightly around him.

"Hey," John's voice is soft in my ear. "You okay?"

I nod, but I'm not sure that I am. "I didn't hurt you, did I? It was good?"

I don't know where this sudden bout of insecurity is coming from, but the thought of me hurting him drives a spike of fear into my heart.

John gathers my head in his hands and lifts it.

I meet his eyes, search them for the truth.

"Thank you," he says. "Thank you for giving me that. For showing me how it could be, how it should be." He smiles, and it's so full of tenderness my eyes begin to sting.

"I want you," I say, which probably sounds crazy to him because we're both spent, and my cock's still twitching. But John just nods. He knows exactly what I mean. He always does.

"Me too," he says and kisses me gently. "I want to be with you too."

John pulls me down to the mattress and, I curl into his side, his arm tight around my back, his hand on my hip.

I rest my head on his shoulder and close my eyes, sighing with contentment.

"We should grab a shower before we both pass out," he mumbles.

"Yeah," I agree.

Neither of us makes a move. I must doze off for a bit because, when I open my eyes and look up, John is standing next to the bed.

"You were out cold for a minute, there," he says, smiling at me. "Come on, Nightingale, let's get cleaned up."

I follow John's hard, rounded ass into the bathroom, smirking at the red handprint I've left on his left cheek. The bathroom is tight for two grown men, but the tub is big enough.

John pulls back the curtain and starts the shower, adjusting the temperature until he's satisfied. He steps into the tub and holds a hand out to me.

"Careful," he says as I step over the edge.

John looks ridiculously good wet.

All I can do is stare as he reaches around me to pull the curtain closed, making sure it's inside with us because he clearly has a functioning brain.

I am useless. I mean, fuck.

He's so hot.

John grins down at me as if he can read my mind. Maybe he can. He grabs a bottle of body wash from a nook above my head.

"See something you like?"

I nod, mute, and he chuckles.

"You are exceedingly good for my ego." He works up a lather but, instead of smoothing it over his own skin, he reaches for me.

Those big hands are miracle workers, massaging the kinks out of my arms, my legs, and my back as he spins me around to face away from him.

I let my head drop to my chest as he works my glutes, my cock rebounding already. John reaches around to take my rapidly hardening flesh into his soapy hand, and I have to brace my hands against the wall. God. Look... I have a very healthy libido, but this is something else. I've never been like this with anyone.

John brushes his lips against my shoulder, then his teeth scrape lightly over my skin. When my head falls back onto him, he sinks those sharp teeth into my muscle there. My knees nearly give. And like I didn't just come less than twenty minutes ago, I'm as hard as a standing stone.

John turns us so that I'm under the spray of water.

I gaze up at his face. There's a grin tugging up the side of his mouth.

"What?"

He shakes his head. "Where did you come from?"

"I could ask you the same," I say, letting the water wash the soap from my body. My cock bobs eagerly between us, and John's perks up to say hello.

I grab the body wash and lather him up, paying particular attention to his dangly bits.

"I really want to try," he says as we rinse off, his voice a grumble. "Would you want to? Are you...?"

"Yes," I nod. "Please." I know I'm begging, but the need to have him inside me has become an imperative. It's as if all the weeks and months of wanting him or trying *not* to want him, have coalesced into an incessant need.

I turn to the wall.

"In here?" He asks, uncertain, though his hands are already on my ass. "I don't have anything."

"We don't need anything," I counter, panting. I feel myself

opening already, anticipating him. Somewhere in my fuzzy brain, though, I remember how thick he is.

"Well," I backtrack. "Maybe we do."

He chuckles. "Hang on."

Before I realize what's happening, there's a whoosh of cold air at my back. I hear John hopscotching into the bedroom, hissing from the cold, no doubt. He's back in seconds, and I laugh.

"Eager much?"

"I want inside you," he says, already flicking open the bottle of lube.

I brace my hands on the wall, away from the water, and stick my ass out for him.

"Do you have any idea how beautiful you are? Fuck. Look at you, so ready for me."

"John..."

"Hang on, baby."

I feel him slide his dick up and down my crease, searching for my puckered ring, and I spread my legs further.

"Tell me if I'm hurting you," he says. "Please, don't let me hurt you."

I nod. "Okay, promise."

"Okay," he says, and I can hear his hesitation.

I press back into him and feel the head of his cock notched against me. I push myself onto him, and, just as I thought, he slips in easily. It's tight and a little uncomfortable, but I can already feel my body relaxing around him.

"Oh, fuck," he groans low and long.

I reach back and put one hand on his thigh to guide him. Slowly, so slowly, I circle my hips, pulling him into me, centimeter by centimeter. Our skin is slippery from the water and the lube. We're hot and slick, and we fit so perfectly.

John is hunched over me, his thighs flexing against the backs of mine. His breath in my ear.

The stretch, it burns, and it feels so fucking good. He invades my channel, and I want to surrender, I do. I will myself to relax even more, and then he's there.

He's right fucking there.

My head falls back onto his shoulder, and his arm comes around my waist. We're locked together, and everything just stops.

There's only the pounding in my chest and the pulse of him inside me. The thundering beat of his heart against my back, and the singing of the shower. It's...heaven.

"Frankie," John breathes into my wet hair.

He gives a tentative, unsure roll of his hips.

I'm going to lose my mind. I'm going to lose my fucking mind.

John's arm tightens around my chest. "Jesus, you feel...it's so tight, you're...God, Frankie."

I can't form words. I'm fuller than I've ever been, stretched and aching with a pleasure I can barely process.

With his next stroke, John alters his position, brushing across my gland and holy...shit. I'm so close to coming already, I'm stunned. I make a noise I've never made before, in my whole bloody life.

John's hands drop to my hips as pace increases, his grip desperate. He has his mouth pressed to the top of my spine, and grunts with every push of his hips. Chanting my name again, and again. Whispering it into my skin like a prayer.

"So good," he's saying. "So fucking good, Frankie...Frankie."

"Johnny..."

I wrap a hand around my dick and stroke in time with his thrusts.

"I'm not going to last long," I warn him.

"Oh, fuck. Come. Just come, I want to feel you squeezing me. You will, won't you, baby? You're gonna milk me, aren't you?"

God, the dirty talk is crazy hot. "Yes," I pant. "Yes, right now."

"Right fucking now?" He asks, slamming into me over and over. Tearing me the fuck up.

I'm so open to him, so eager to receive him.

"Yes," I hiss. "Yes, now. Now...now...now..." I come with a strangled cry, splashing wall of the shower with my release. My ass flexes, my thigh muscles shake as I crash and spiral and burn.

John makes a guttural noise that bounces off the tiled walls, and then I am flooded with warmth, his release filling every nook and cranny. It's such an incredible sensation and knowing that it's him, that's it's John, I want to cry and smile and laugh all at once.

My knees are weak. I'm shaking, held up by John, who doesn't seem to have full control over his body either. We're swaying like branches in the wind.

John kisses the side of my neck and chuckles under his breath.

"You're going to be the death of me, I think," he says, his voice warm with affection. He caresses me with slick fingers, soothing me as he slips free of my body.

We rinse off quickly and stagger back to bed, sated and grinning. John gathers me close, and I'm content to be wrapped up in him.

That he can't seem to keep his hands - or lips - off me makes me unreasonably happy. I can't stop smiling.

"Good?" He asks, brushing my drying hair out of my face.

"More than," I mumble. And then I'm out like a spent match.

10

I've never been one of those glass-half-full types, but shit. My glass is pretty fucking full at the moment.

I have a job I love, and a man I can't keep my hands off of. What's more, he can't keep his hands off me.

John's been a very quick study. He's learned my body so well, what I like and what makes me drool and babble and shake, I think he knows me better than I do.

But it's more than the sex - which is phenomenal, I can't stress that enough – it's him. His kindness, his strength, the way he listens to me.

He doesn't think I'm crazy when I stop, mid-sentence, to point out the song that's playing in the restaurant while we eat. He doesn't get angry when I drag him to a flea market to search for buried treasure in the form of old vinyl. He doesn't complain about driving down to the city, where we spend most of our time together.

John Burton is as close to perfect as they come...except for one thing.

Every once in a while, he'll disappear for a day or two. At first, I assume it's for work or for Lexi but, when I ask, he dodges the question or distracts me with sex.

Really outstanding fucking sex.

And then there are the texts. The random calls.

They come at all hours of the day and night, and always seem to alter his mood. Never for the better.

"Is everything alright?" I always ask.

"Yep," is his standard reply.

It makes me think about the months he disappeared from my life without a word. Granted, we weren't much to each other back then, but it had still hurt. Having had him at the center of my world these last few months, in my bed and, yes, in my heart, I'm terrified he'll disappear again.

We're at his place tonight, sitting on his concrete slab of a balcony, looking out over a quiet, suburban highway. The only thing romantic about this scene is the man whose lap I currently occupy.

His hand strokes up and down my naked thigh, from my knee to where my briefs begin. We're curled in a thick blanket on this unusually warm, Sunday night in November when his phone buzzes beside him.

John picks it up. I feel his body jolt beneath mine, muscles going rigid.

"What's wrong?"

His breathing changes, sawing in and out of his chest, and I can feel his heart thudding against my back. It's a déjà vu moment if I've ever had one.

"John?"

"I need to go," he says, practically pushing me off his lap.

The chilled air prickles my skin. I quickly gather the discarded blanket around me and follow him back inside his flat.

"John, what's going on? Is it Lexi?"

"I'm sorry," he says, jumping into a pair of jeans. He pulls a sweater over his head and jams his feet into a pair of sneakers. "Have you seen my keys?"

"John, talk to me," I plead, an icy finger of fear slicing into my gut. "Maybe I can help this time."

"You can't," he snaps angrily, frantically searching the table by the door for his car keys.

My stomach sinks when I hear the tell-tale jingle.

John grabs his coat from the rack and swings the door open, glancing only briefly at me over his shoulder.

"I'll be back," he says, breathless. "I...I'm sorry."

And then he's gone.

I stand there for a moment, too stunned and too hurt to move. I think I expect him to walk back through the door, remembering that he has me in his life now. That I'm here for him, and I'm willing to share whatever burdens he has.

He must know this.

I pull the blanket tighter around me and plop down on the sofa. It's lumpy and uncomfortable, and I wish I were at home. I have half a mind to get dressed, get in my car, and drive back to Philly. Fuck all of this.

But something has happened, something that has John rattled. I can't help but want to be here for him when he gets back, no matter how angry I am.

We need to talk about whatever it is that always has him checking his phone, frowning when it chimes with a message from God knows who. Was he racing to see Lexi right now? To Doylestown? To his ex-wife?

TO Patrick?

The name enters my mind before I can stop it.

Patrick. The only other man John has ever felt anything for. Patrick, the teacher from John's old school.

His old school.

I reach for my backpack, opening it and pulling out my laptop. I fire it up and wait for it to connect to John's Wi-Fi.

What I'm about to do is invasive, I know, but...

I open a browser, head to Google, and type in *Walt Whitman High School, Pennsylvania*. I can't remember the name of the town and don't bother to get up and go look at the photograph.

A few results pop up, and I scan them until I see Edgerton. That's the place. There are several articles about the football team, one about the debate team. I find the school's directory and look through it for a 'Patrick.' There are three.

None of them jump out at me, so I change my search.

John Burton, Walt Whitman High School, Patrick

There are dozens of results, but that's not what stops me cold. It's the question glaring at me from the top of my screen.

Did you mean Michael John Dalton? We're showing results for Michael John Dalton. Click here to search for John Burton.

John Dalton? Michael?

What the shit?

I scroll down to look for photos, and... Fuck.

There he is.

John.

My John.

Dalton, not Burton.

Michael, not John, smiling in front of a bunch of kids, his arm around a handsome blonde man with a shy smile and a thin frame.

Michael John Dalton.

I scroll further and stop, not really able to wrap my head around the headlines for these articles.

LOCAL HIGH SCHOOL TEACHER ARRESTED ON SUSPICION OF SEX WITH STUDENT

TEACHER CLAIMS INNOCENCE IN SCHOOL SEX SCANDAL

AUTHORITIES STRUGGLE TO BUILD CASE AGAINST ALLEGED SEX OFFENDER AS VICTIM PROTESTS CHARGES

My stomach roils violently and I rush to the loo, reaching it just in time to start retching uncontrollably.

After wiping my mouth with the back of my hand, I slink to the floor by the (blessedly cleanish) toilet, unable to move. I lean my forehead against the lip of the bathtub, grateful for the silence and for its cold surface against my overheated skin. The room spins around me. I can't stop fucking shaking.

Not John, I keep thinking. *Not my John.*

Somehow, after who knows how long, I'm eventually able to

stand. I rinse my mouth in the sink and make my way back to the living room. The laptop has gone to sleep in my absence, and I touch the space bar to wake it up.

LOCAL TEACHER FIRED AFTER SCANDAL ROCKS WHITMAN HIGH

Jesus Christ.

I scroll down and find one story that has a video. Reluctantly, hands shaking so badly I can barely get them to do my bidding, I click.

The woman in the video is about sixty years old. She's barely taller than the podium in front of her, and she clings to it with both hands. A cluster of microphones is mounted in front like a murder of crows, waiting to capture her every word. The lobby is shabby, two-star hotel shabby, with drab vertical blinds that hang in dull windows.

Next to the woman, there's a younger woman in a suit, about thirty-five, and a teenaged boy.

I stare at the boy, and my gut twists with rage. *How could he? How could anyone...?*

Tearing my eyes from his sweet, sad face, I finally notice the banner on the screen below them. It reads *Whitman High School victim's family speaks in defense of accused teacher.*

Wait. What?

Hurriedly, I click play.

"*Michael John Dalton is innocent,*" the older woman begins. "*My family has said this over and over, and yet this witch hunt continues. We're so saddened by it. We're confused by it. And we're angry because no one seems to care about the truth, and this man – this good man – is suffering for it.*"

"*But Ms. Taylor,*" one reporter says, his suit as ill-fitting as his toupe. "*Mr. Dalton was caught with your grandson, in his car, by school police.*" The man's tone drips with innuendo.

Ms. Taylor grits her teeth. "*Doing what?*" She asks, her tone indignant. "*Comforting a child who was upset. Since when is that a crime?*"

"*They were caught in a ...embrace. And isn't it true that your grandson is gay?"* The reporter tosses the words out like daggers. Mother-fucking wanker.

Camera flashes pop incessantly, and there's a murmur amongst the school of sharks. Clearly, they smell blood.

My own blood heats as the truth of the situation begins to take shape.

"What does that matter?" Ms. Taylor snaps back.

"And Mr. Dalton himself has all but admitted his homosex-"

"Again, what the heck does that have to do with anything?" The boy's grandmother practically vibrates with her indignation.

Beside her, the younger woman wrings her hands and makes a feeble attempt to redirect the focus of the gathered horde.

"Please allow Ms. Taylor to finish her statement."

The teen is clearly miserable, but he fumes. He eyes the crowd of reporters like he wants to tear them apart with his bare hands. I'm right there with him.

Ms. Taylor holds up her hand when the members of the press begin to shout at once.

"This boy, my grandson, is standing up here telling you that nothing untoward happened between him and Michael John Dalton. I am telling you nothing happened. But you all don't care about that, you have a juicy story for your ratings and your newspapers. Shame on you!" She's strong in her convictions, anyone with eyes can see it. I see it, and I feel the same. Whoever he is, John – Michael John – he isn't capable of doing what they've accused him of.

"Then how can you explain-"

"I'd just found out my little sister has cancer!" The teen screams, star-tling the room. His face is red with his fury, his fists clenched at his side. Beside him, his grandmother closes her eyes and reaches for one of his hands. He clasps it. *"Why can't you leave us all alone? Mr. Dalton ain't done nothing wrong. You're all horrible to treat him like this. Chasing him around and picketing his house. He's a good teacher. He cares."*

The video cuts back to an in-studio reporter. They run footage of John being led to a police car in handcuffs. He looks helpless and confused, gobsmacked. My heart clenches for him.

Closing my eyes, I take a deep breath and return to the article. At the bottom of the screen, the words *LOCAL TEACHER EXONERATED*, scroll across, but they clearly aren't treating him like he's innocent.

There's more footage of John leaving a courthouse, presumably after the charges were dismissed. They show him wading through a mob of protesters and a sea of hateful, homophobic signs. Someone throws a bottle at him as he's led down the steps and into a waiting SUV.

I think back to our day at the flea market, and how he reacted to those assholes in the Camaro, and sigh. No wonder he responded the way he did. Then again, he hadn't told me any of this. Anger and sympathy are at war in my chest.

I click back to the search results and scroll down.

EDGERTON SCHOOL DISTRICT DENIES REINSTATEMENT OF EXONERATED TEACHER

Jesus.

ANOTHER WHITMAN TEACHER OUSTED AS PARENTS COMPLAIN ABOUT HIS 'INAPPROPRIATE LIFESTYLE'

I click the link and, sure enough, it's the blond man from the photo. Patrick Fosse.

This is all so much to take in, I don't begin to know how to deal with it. I'm angry with the entire state of Pennsylvania on John's behalf. I want to hug and kiss Ms. Taylor and her poor grandchildren. A big part of me wants to pull John into my arms and shield him from everything and everyone that would ever wish him harm.

Another part wants to punch John in the face for not trusting me with any of this. And... There it is. That's what hurts – so much. He doesn't trust me.

This is the thought in my head as I collapse back against the sofa cushions. I stare up at John's sad, popcorn ceiling until I drift off into an exhausted, dreamless sleep.

***

When I wake, I find I'm stretched out along the couch and a blanket has been draped over me. Sunlight streams in through the balcony doors. On the table, the laptop is closed. I don't remember closing it.

"John?" My throat is rough from all the retching and crying and worrying and fuming.

"I'm here." His voice reaches out from the corner of the room that's still in shadow.

I sit up, feeling like I've been hit by a cement lorry.

John is slumped in a chair, staring at me. His eyes blaze in the dark, but I can't make out his expression.

I don't know what to say to him. All of the hurt and rage and fear come slithering back, but mostly I'm worried about him. And about us.

"You could have told me." I dive right into the deep end. I don't know if he's seen what I'd been doing online, but I figure there's no reason for *me* to lie, at least.

"I changed my name because I couldn't get hired for anything, not anywhere within driving distance. When I went into construction, I took my mother's maiden name as my new last name. Legally. But even then, I would get harassed. At shops, at restaurants. Too many people knew my face, knew the story – or their version of it. I became a recluse in my own hometown. I couldn't make a damn living."

I nod and try to keep my voice even. "I'm sorry you had to leave a job you loved, the place you grew up," I say, and I mean it.

"Thank you," he replies. I can hear the gratitude in his voice. The hope.

"Where did you go last night? Where do you go?"

"To Children's Hospital," he says, his voice is scratchy with fatigue. He's been up all night, and it shows. His clothes are rumpled, there's two days' growth on his chin, and his hair is a mess. Like he's been clutching at it. "I helped Lexi and her grandmother move out here to Philly a few months ago, so she could be closer to the specialist."

"Lexi is the sister of the boy that...?"

"Lance. Yes." John's voice cracks a little. "His baby sister. She's twelve now... That all happened when she was diagnosed with myeloma, bone marrow cancer. I grew close with the family, you see."

I nod.

"And they have limited resources, they couldn't afford Lexi's treatments, even with the insurance. Even if Lance had skipped college and gotten whatever job he could find, they needed help. They need help."

"Niece, though?"

He gives me a sheepish smile. "She's like a niece to me, yes."

"John..." I begin, but he interrupts me.

"How?" He asks, leaning forward to place his elbows on his knees. Even from across the room, I can see the fear in his eyes. "How was I supposed to tell you?"

I shake my head as the anger decides to return. "You could have just opened your mouth and told me, I would have believed you. Believed in you."

"And now you don't?"

"I'm not saying that." I snap. Sigh. Sit up. My head throbs at my temples, and I run a rough hand over my face. I just want to sink into my bed and play *Anastasis* on repeat.

Listening to Dead Can Dance is like dropping acid. Or how I presume it would be. My inner monologue is nonsensical.

"What are you saying, Frankie? Can you honestly tell me you would have believed me? Believed that I'd never touched Lance inappropriately, that I hadn't lured him to my car and preyed upon him? That the school official that *discovered* us..." He uses air quotes. "... wasn't a homophobic asshat? It's a lot to swallow. A lot."

"But, I would have!" He winces at my outburst. I want to scream the paint off the walls. "You didn't give me the bloody chance to, though. Did you? What was the point of all this – of us - if you can't trust me?"

Needing to move, I get up and start pacing. I need to not look at him for a while. Need to not be here. It's too risky for me to go to the station. I don't want a lot of questions about why I look like shit, 'cause I know I do. I debate driving back down to Philly, even though it's not a good idea in my current frame of mind.

This is why I'm not cut out for relationships. I'm blinded too easily. And with John, I'd given more of myself than ever. Every bit of me. Yet, he'd kept this from me for months.

God, I hurt. I walk to the bedroom to get dressed.

John follows but keeps his distance. "Please, don't go." His voice, usually so rich and full, is thin and reedy.

"You can't expect me to stay here, John...Michael...whatever your name is," I retort, pulling on my jeans. "It's not fair. You can't do that to me."

"I don't want to be fair, I want you here." It's probably the most honest thing he's ever said to me, but I can't deal with it. "Stay with me, Nightingale, let me explain. I... I love you."

That fucking stops me in my tracks. I whirl on him.

"Really? You say that *now*? That's fucking rich. And it's cruel to tell me that. Now? Right now?" Right at this moment, when I'm so raw, I'm bleeding on the inside. How dare he? "*This* is when you choose to tell me you fucking love me? I asked you. I asked you if there was anything I needed to know, and you said no. You said... You..."

I'm finding it hard to speak, hard to breathe. If I don't leave right now, I'm going to start sobbing again.

He takes a step toward me. "Frankie-"

I hold up a hand, hating the fact that it wobbles. "Don't. Who even are you?"

To his credit, John does stop but only a foot or so away from me. If I stretched out my arm, I could touch him. Grab him. Yank him to me and make him kiss me, touch me, fuck this hurt away. But I don't.

I can't.

I'm not even sure I know this man, *Michael John Dalton*.

But then he's staring at me like he's about to fly apart at the seams.

My heart can't help but break for him. He genuinely cares for me. It's written all over his face, but... Just thinking of everything I don't know about him sends sharp pain shooting through my abdomen.

"I need time. To think."

He nods eagerly. "Okay, of course. Yes. Whatever you need just... Please..."

"I'll..." I try to swallow and end up coughing. "I-I'll call you."

I snatch up the rest of my things, and then I walk out of John's bedroom. Out of his life.

Out of this nightmare.

M usic truly is a balm.

  I spend the rest of the weekend ignoring my mobile phone and drowning in Sigur Ros and a pricey bottle of Scotch I'd picked up the last time I went to visit my family.

When I get to the station the Monday night, I turn off the phone lines and indulge my pain. I slide into it, let it have its greedy way with me. It's delicious, in a perverted, self-destructive sense. A self-fulfilling prophecy.

When I call Dyer and ask him to sit in on my shift, he only hesitates for a moment before agreeing. His eyes grow comically wide when he walks into the booth and sees my face.

"Trouble in paradise?" He settles into the chair on the other side of the desk. John's chair.

I cue up *Stinkfist* by Tool and slump back into my seat. The phones blink nonstop. I ignore them.

"Damn," he whispers. "That bad?"

I only grunt in response and program a digital block of songs and station idents that will carry me through the next hour. I can't even be arsed to fire up the turntables tonight. For the first time ever, I don't want to be here.

"Talk," Dyer demands, and I do. I tell him everything.

By the time I'm done, there's a vein ticking in his forehead. I don't think I've ever seen him this angry.

"Holy...fuck." He slides his chair closer. Reaching across the desk, he takes my hand and squeezes it.

"And after all of that, he said he fucking *loves* you?"

"That's not what I'm focusing on right now," I mutter. I know, if I do, I'll lose this rage. And I have every right to it.

"Damn right, you do," Dyer says when I tell him this. "But..."

"No *buts*."

Dyer shushes me. "He loves you, or so he says. You haven't told me how you feel about him."

"About who? John Burton or Michael John Dalton?" I bark. "Michael John Dalton is an innocent man accused of a heinous crime, drummed out of a town and a profession he loved because people are so closed-minded and hungry for a scandal, they'll make one up just because they can."

This pours out of me in one continuous sentence. Once I start, I can't seem to stop talking.

"Michael John Dalton was there for a kid who needed a friend and nearly got railroaded for it. John *Burton* is a contractor and a substitute teacher. He's a guy I've been fucking around with for the last few months, but I know nothing about John Burton. Not really."

Dyer gives me a look like I'm full of shit.

"John is the guy that's had you floating on air these last few months," he says. "He's the guy that's made you so happy, your entire body language has changed. He's the guy you talk about non-fucking-stop when we're hanging out, which has been less and less of late *because* of John. Who the fuck cares what his last name is? Or, you know, his first?"

Dyer levels his *I-dare-you-to-fight-me-on-this* look at me.

I don't want to hold his gaze, but I do.

"You need to decide if you can forgive him for keeping this from you. If you can love him despite it because – baby - no matter what you say, you are stupid in love with that man."

"I care about him," I counter, and then sigh, dropping my head into my free hand. "Fuck, D. What the hell do I do?"

Dyer releases my hand and sits back in his chair. "Maybe think about what *you* would have done in his place. Was he planning to tell you down the road? Did you even ask?"

I hadn't, and Dyer sees this on my face.

"Thought not," he scolds. "I'm not saying what he did was right, it's ten different flavors of wrong, but..."

"I need to let him explain," I finish for him.

"You need to let him explain. You need to tell him how you feel, all of it – the love, the pain – all of it. And then you need to either find a way forward with him or walk away for good."

Fresh pain blooms in my chest, centered around my heart.

Could I even do that? Walk away?

***

I've exhausted my knowledge of breakup songs by the time Friday rolls around, and yet manage to lean into my melancholy with tracks from Black Tape for a Blue Girl, Miranda Sex Garden, and Fever Ray, with a little Brendan Perry for good measure. The phones have been blinking non-stop. I don't care. There's no way I can translate someone else's mood into music when I'm down in the shit like this.

Every time I come in for my shift, I expect to find a note from Nicki, but she leaves me alone. Maybe I've earned some leeway. We'll see how long it lasts.

John hasn't tried to call or text me for three days. Maybe he's given up. When my phone vibrates on the desk, some traitorous part of me hopes it's him.

"Fuck off," I say to myself. I'm too soft. Still, I glance at the screen because even seeing his name brings a warmth to my belly.

It isn't John, though. It's Garrett.

Shocked, I picked up the call. "G?"

"What the fuck is going on with you, Frankie?"

"I...what?"

"I know you're moody, but this new wave, emo shit is getting old."

I pull the phone away from my ear and double-check the caller ID. "Garrett?"

He sighs. "Of course, it's me. What's going on, are you okay?"

"I'm fine," I say, still stunned to hear his voice. "Are you listening to my set?"

"I usually do."

"What? No, you don't." I am indignant. "You hate my show."

"Franklin." Garrett sighs again, as if we've had this argument a million times.

We've had a million arguments, but never this one. Garrett despises my show. Loathes the station. I know this. I *know* it.

"Despite what you may think, I never hated your show, or the station. I just think you can do better."

And, there it is. "I'm not in the mood to defend my life choices tonight, Garrett."

"What's the matter, love?" His voice has gone soft and suddenly fresh tears spring to my eyes. "And don't say nothing. Just because we're not together anymore doesn't mean I don't know you better than most."

"It's really nothing." My voice falters and I clear my throat. "Really."

"Doesn't sound like nothing," he counters. "You sound...heartbroken."

I hiccup, choking back a sob.

"Oh, Frankie..."

I hear rustling and know he's settling in for a conversation I don't know I want to have with him. Not with him.

And yet, when I open my mouth, everything spills out. Everything.

How John and I met. How we grew closer and closer before he disappeared. How he came back and we fell into a weird are-we-or-aren't-we-dating situation. How he asked me out and everything since. By the time I get to the bit about Edgerton, and the ordeal he went through there, I'm out of breath. My cheeks are wet and my eyes are blurry.

I swipe at my face and double check the amount of time left in the block of songs I've pre-programmed.

"Wow," Garrett says. "Just, wow. I don't think I've ever heard you like this."

"Like what?"

"Affected," he replies after a beat. "Frankie, you really care about this guy."

"Of course, I do!" I am exasperated. "But it's all a lie."

"What's all a lie?"

"Us. Him." I push a hand through my hair and my thumb catches on a tangled curl. I yank until I free myself, wincing, but the pain calms me down a little.

"Do I need to tell you how ridiculous that sounds?"

I'm pouting and he can't even see me. "You only have the liner notes."

"So, tell me what I'm missing."

I deflate, sinking further into the captain's chair. "How do I trust him after this?"

"Babes...I know it's shitty that he didn't tell you," Garrett says, sounding irritatingly reasonable. "It sounds like things are pretty serious between you, and he should have been honest."

"Exactly."

"On the other hand," he continues, interrupting me. "I don't know what I would have done in his situation."

"You wouldn't have kept something this important from me," I argue. "You never lied to me, Garrett. You never would."

Silence stretches on between us, and I feel vindicated. When Garrett speaks again, he sounds almost chastened.

"Some things," he begins after a long minute. "Some things are... difficult to share with the people you care about. Sometimes *because* you care about someone, you want to avoid hurting them. And so, you...you..."

"You lie?"

"Did John lie?"

I think about that. "About his name, he did."

"You said he changed it," Garrett countered. "That's not a lie. I mean, if I'd changed my name, I wouldn't go around announcing it."

"I guess not." I marinate on that for a bit. I don't know what I'd do under the circumstances, but I like to think I wouldn't keep something so huge from someone I was involved with.

"The question you really need to ask, the most important one anyway, is whether he's worth it. Worth your forgiveness." I hear him shift on the other end of the call. "'Cause, babes, you can play it down all you want. You feel something for this guy, something real, or it wouldn't be tearing you up like this."

"I mean...I care."

He chuckles softly. "You more than care, you've played *She Wants Revenge* every night this week." A small laugh, a pause. "I have to say, I'm a little jealous."

"Garrett," I warn.

"No, no. I know. We had our time, but..." He exhales. "Whoever this John guy is, he has you in a way I never did. In a way I don't think I ever could."

"That's not-"

"It is." I can almost hear his smile through the phone. "And it's ok. I'm happy for you. You deserve to fall hard for someone, as long as they fall hard for you."

If he'd asked me a week ago, I would have said yeah. John and I were on the same page. Now?

"I don't know what to do, G." I hate how small I sound.

"Yeah, you do, love," he chides softly. "You have to trust your instincts. When have they ever let you down?"

My instinct is to curl into a ball and cry, but Garrett's right about one thing. He knows me.

"I'll let you get back to it," he says.

"Thanks for calling."

"Thanks for answering."

I frown at that, then realize we hadn't spoken in a while. We'd said we'd try to stay friends, but I'd been so wrapped up in John, I'd neglected everyone else. I still love Garrett. I'm not in love with him, but I still love him. I want us to be friends.

I don't say any of this, but I don't think I need to. He gets me. In this way, he gets me.

"Play something for me."

"What's your mood?" A smile tugs at my lips. Amazing.

Garrett hums into the phone before answering. "Let's go with *reformed.*"

I laugh. It's the first genuine laugh I've had all week.

"Goodnight, G."

I hang up the phone and add *Should Have Known Better* by Sufjan Stevens to the queue.

12

It's another week before I work up the courage to text John. I don't call him, prolonging the moment before I hear his voice again. I don't think I'd make it through a telephone call without breaking down. I text and tell him to come over at the weekend.

No surprise, I've been a mess. Even the girls have noticed me slinking around our flat. They've been inordinately attentive, checking in on me when they leave in the morning for school and when they get home in the afternoon.

Hmmmph. I guess they're not so bad.

Nicki pulls me into her office one evening, after I arrive for my shift, to ask if everything's okay. Apparently, my listeners have complained about not being able to get through the phone lines. I've been forcing mine down their throats, and that needs to stop. Nicki doesn't say this last bit, but I know it.

It's two Saturday mornings removed from that fateful weekend when John rings my buzzer.

I think I've braced myself to see him, but when I open the door, all the blood in my veins begins to fizzle.

He looks beautiful. And awful. Dark circles have formed under his eyes. His hair is a little greasy, and I don't think he's shaved since I last saw him. The beard actually suits him. The hair not so much.

"I was beginning to think I'd never hear from you again." His voice is a shadow of itself, gravelly and yet thin. It rubs over my raw nerves and makes my heart ache.

I widen the door and gesture him inside, catching his scent as he shuffles past me. Before I know it, I've closed the door and grabbed him from behind. I bury my face in the back of his jacket and band my arms around his torso, clutching him to me. I've missed him so fucking bad.

He freezes, and slowly brings his hands up to cover my bare arms. Goosebumps explode across my entire body, every hair on end.

John turns and pulls, gathering me close, and I let him. Too relieved to be inside the circle of his embrace again to fight it.

"I'm so fucking sorry, baby," he whispers into my hair as he clutches me tight. "God, you'll never know how sorry I am."

I do know. I've always known, even before he came back to his flat that night and found that I'd learned the truth about him. I knew he'd regret not telling me.

Time slips by as we stand in my doorway. Eventually, I slip out of his arms and lead him over to the couch.

He sits close, his hand on my leg. It's like he can't stand the thought of losing contact with me, and I feel the same. Even if I don't like needing him this much at the moment.

"How's Lexi?"

My question brings a sad smile to his face. "She's...very ill, awake now, but comfortable. Thank you for asking."

"And...her bills? You're still helping with those?"

He nods. "Yes, as much as I can."

"Why?" I ask, and he frowns a little.

"I told you, the family, they can't..."

"But you're not family," I say. "You're a victim. You did nothing wrong. You owe no one."

"I..." He looks at me, searching for the words to explain what I've already guessed. "They need help. I can help. I don't have anyone, anything, just my rent. My car is paid off. The shop basically runs itself. " He shrugs, as if it's the most natural thing in the world, caring for a family that isn't his own.

"I help because I can." He searches my eyes. "Because family should be there for you. Mine isn't. Theirs' wasn't then and isn't now. And mine..." He exhales. "We've become family to each other. They need me."

He says it as if it's the most simple, logical thing in the world.

It's at this moment I realize I am deeply, irrevocably in love with this man. It hits me like a bloody freight train, how important he's become to me. I want him.

I want him, I want him, I want him.

I exhale a shuddering breath. "You can't keep anything else from me, I don't care what it is."

Surprised, John's mouth drops open. His eyes shine with tentative hope and incredulous joy.

"Frankie..." he whispers and slides closer to me. Stronger, he declares, "I... I won't. Not ever again. God, I promise."

"We're in it together, right? This...thing we have, it's..." My heart thunders inside my ribcage.

"Together, yes." He grabs my hands and grips them tightly. "Frankie..."

"I love you too," I say and, fuck. The smile he gives me... I could live on it alone.

"Baby," he whispers and cups my face in his hands. "Say it again. Please."

"Don't fucking lie to me again," I growl, still angry but so in love with this guy. So in awe of his big, stupid heart, I can't see straight.

He gives his head a vigorous shake. "I promise. Please-"

I lean forward and kiss him, my head swimming with the possibilities of us. Can we really move past this? Is it really even a question?

"I'm so mad at you," I whisper between kisses, gripping his shoulders so hard, I know I'm leaving bruises. "But, I fucking love you, Michael John Dalton."

"Burton," he corrects me, but his eyes are liquid.

"Whoever you are," I promise. "I love you."

"I love you so much, Nightingale." He shakes his head. "No more secrets."

"Good," I scold, holding onto the last threads of my ire. "Because I need you."

"Thank fucking god," he says, finally pulling me into his lap and capturing my mouth again.

I let myself sink into it this time.

John breaks off, breathless. "By the way, I've been listening to your overnights. Can we talk about the depressing-as-hell music you've been playing?"

"Yeah," I say, running my fingers through his hair. It's kinda gross. "And whose fucking fault is that?"

EPILOGUE

Happily-ever-after is a fairy tale. It's the closing shot of a rom-com. The slogan at a high school prom.

In the four months that John and I have been together, there's been a lot of joy and a little sorrow. Under the care of her new doctors, Lexi is much better, but she's not out of the woods just yet.

John and I? We're solid.

We've gotten to a place where *ever-after* is a very real possibility, but it takes work. I've never felt so wholly myself as I do when I'm with him.

Not that I need him to make me whole, I've just learned more about myself. Who I am and what I have to offer. I've learned how to see what John sees when he looks at me.

I want to ask him to move in.

Yeah, I know. Right?

Philly isn't practical for him, and Doylestown isn't convenient for me, so I'm not sure where we would even live, but I'm hoping we'll figure that out.

First, though, I need to work up the courage to ask him. And pray to whatever gods that are out there he says yes. That I'll get a Christmas miracle.

Today is Sunday, and Nicki has invited everyone to a celebratory brunch at Rick's Pub. WKMP is fifteen years old this week, and the whole crew comes in for the event. The station is on autopilot for the afternoon, allowing the entire staff to attend.

Dyer's here, as are Gayle and her daughter, Simon and his latest conquest, Mario, and Kathy.

It's freezing outside. There's day-old snow on the ground, and tiny ice cubes falling from the cloudy sky, but inside is toasty and warm. The food is hot, and the drinks are cold, it's perfect.

John and I share a high-top table near the windows, and I scan the room, taking in the crowd. There are a lot of locals here, quite a few of them station-listeners. Occasionally one will wander over to tell me how much they enjoy my show.

I try not to blush.

John nudges my shoulder when one woman tells me she earned her bachelor's degree listening to me while she studied.

"You were a lifesaver," she gushes, squeezing my arm.

"That's great," I say, pleased for her. "Congratulations. Do you know what you're going to do now?"

"I've applied for a position in the school district."

"That's fantastic," John says, and I look over at him. He's smiling, but I can see the regret in his eyes.

"There's such a shortage of qualified teachers right now," she tells us.

After she walks away, I turn to him. "You know," I start softly. "You could get your certification and go full-time. Sounds like they need you."

He shakes his head. "No, I don't think so."

"You don't believe that you could, or you don't want to?"

"I...I just..."

"What are you afraid of, John? Someone finding out what happened to you?"

"I have a company to run, Frankie." He turns his face back to the crowd.

"Nothing is stopping you from moving that to part-time, maybe on the weekends or something." I've been working on my argument for a while. There's no real reason for him not to teach full-time. "Babe, you were born to stand in front of a classroom, not hang drywall."

"Why are you pushing this?" He asks, turning back to me. There's no anger, only confusion.

"Why are you so keen on not doing something you so clearly love?" I ask, grasping his hand under the table. "I know you, Johnny. You're an educator."

He shrugs.

"Surely, you could get your records transferred over in your new name."

"I did. I have, but I'm a substitute. I can fly under the radar. If I went full-time..." He rubs the back of his neck. "What if...? What if someone – a student or a parent - looks into my past?"

"What past?" I ask and take his chin in my hand. I wait until he meets my eyes. "You didn't do anything wrong. Nothing. And there are a million people who could testify to that, including Lexi and Lance and nana Taylor."

"I don't know," he says, but I can see the wheels turning. He frowns, but a tiny smile curves his lips. "Nana Taylor?"

"She reminds me of my Gran." I smile, and he returns it fully.

He introduced me to Ms. Taylor and Lexi a few weeks after we got back together. After only a few hours with them, I got it. They're wonderful. And they're wonderful to him. For him. I've fallen in love with the lot of them.

Lance is whip-smart and doing well in his residency at a teaching hospital. The kid is so grateful to John, it's heartwarming. And it's clear he looks up to him.

"Just think about it, okay? You'd have to move to the school district, right? Not too much of a hardship."

John nods, but I can see the wheels turning.

I ease off because I don't want to push him. If I've learned anything about John over these last months, it's that he needs to come to things in his own time.

John stands and rounds the table, coming up behind me. He wraps his arms around my shoulders and drops his face into my neck before he takes a deep breath.

I hold him to me. This is new, this blatant PDA. New for both of us.

Across the room, I see Nicki talking to the owner of the pub, Rick somebody or other. They look rather cozy, actually. John was right when he said the man was handsome, but he doesn't hold a candle to my brawny lad.

John presses a kiss to the side of my neck.

"Babe?"

"Hmmm?" I lean back into him, loving the feel of him around me.

"Let's get a place together, you and me."

I smile, closing my eyes. "Okay," I say, as casually as I can manage while my insides fizz like champagne.

John's laughter rumbles against my back. "Just like that? Okay?"

"Mmm-hmm," I reply, turning my head to rest my cheek against his chest.

John cups my jaw in his hand and lifts it until I face him. He searches my eyes.

"Really?"

I smile up at him, giddy. "Really."

"Good," he says, ducking his gaze. "Because Rick offered me a deal on his place here in New Bromley, and I kinda took him up on it."

"Okay," I shrug, still smiling.

The kiss he plants on me is swift and instantly consuming.

"Fuck." He groans against my lips. "I have the key if you want to get out of here and take a look." Before I can respond, he kisses me again.

"Right now?" I pant into his mouth when we come up for air. We're not subtle, and I can practically feel the eyes on us. I can almost smell John's arousal. Christ.

"Right now," he says, hot and urgent. He grabs his coat from the back of his chair. "It's just down the street. We can duck out for a little while, yeah?"

My dick is completely onboard with the idea. "Let's go."

As we rush to the door, I catch a glimpse of Garrett out of the corner of my eye. My steps falter for a moment.

He makes a B line straight for Dyer, who looks at him like a deer caught in headlights.

Strange. They didn't really get along when Garrett and I were together.

I want to ask Dyer what's going on, but John grabs my hand, pulling me after him, and I file the investigation away for later.

***

Thank God Rick's old place isn't far. By the time we've stumbled into the vestibule, we're in various stages of undress. My fly is undone, John's shirt is untucked, and we're clawing and biting each other like cannibals.

We fall through the door and into the unfurnished apartment. John kicks blindly behind him.

I send up silent thanks to Rick for leaving the heat on, and for the thick wall-to-wall carpet because I go immediately to my knees in front of John. I work my way inside his trousers and underwear to get to his cock. He's hot and hard in my hand, and so greedy for me.

John shucks his coat and tosses it on the floor behind me.

I palm him, eager to get him in my mouth, but John grabs my jacket and pulls it off. It lands on the floor next to his. Then he's pushing me onto my back, kneeling over me and tugging at my clothes.

I get the hint and strip while he does the same.

And all I can do is writhe and moan. John's on me, hands and mouth everywhere.

"Baby..." I pant up to the cavernous ceiling. "They must be fifteen feet or more. "Wow, this place is fantastic."

"I know," he says, spreading my thighs and dipping his head between my legs. He circles his tongue around the tip of my cock, and I jerk up off the floor.

I hear the tell-tale snick of the cap of a bottle, and then cold liquid drips down my crease. I arch into the touch when I feel John's fingers slide along my pucker.

"Yes," I hiss, not caring why he happens to have a bottle of lube with him.

"Do you like the apartment?" He slides a thick finger inside me, and I gasp at the invasion.

"So far," I manage to say. "Nice carpet. Lots of, *uhnnnn*, natural light."

"Mmm," he mumbles before sliding in a second finger and twisting his hand to find my spot, lighting me up from the inside.

"Oh, bloody *fuck*." Pleasure zings across my nerve endings.

"I love you like this, shaking with need. Ready to come and waiting for me to take you there." His voice is a growl that bounces off the bare walls. "You make me want to do things to you."

Do them all, I think.

The only light in the room filters through the windows, painting John's bare skin with a pinkish, golden glow.

"I need to be in you now, baby." John lines up the head of his bare cock with my entrance, and I use my hands to hold my thighs apart for him.

"I need you there."

He pushes inside without another word, and I moan into the empty room. One smooth stroke, and I'm full of him.

It's quiet, save for our mingling breaths and groans. No sounds of traffic, no people nearby, no music. Not even in my head. There's only Johnny, my John, and a bubble of silence around us.

He sets a brutal but steady rhythm, driving me rapidly toward the finish line.

My cock dribbles nonstop, leaving threads of precome against my stomach.

John wraps one beefy hand around me and strokes my length in time with his thrusts. His other hand is under my ass, and he spreads me wide as he pushes in and out. His eyes lock on the place where our bodies join, his expression positively feral.

"Won't last long," I croak, and he nods, grunting in response.

When he flicks his thumb over my slit, my cock jerks in his hand. I arch and shimmy and squirm as waves of pleasure pulse through me, from the soles of my feet to the crown of my head, and I disintegrate, clenching and releasing and clenching again. The orgasm spirals out from the base of my spine, down my thighs, and up through my balls, spilling over John's fist and causing him to lose his rhythm.

I'm warm, inside and out, spasming around him in seemingly endless bouts of ecstasy.

"You're mine," John growls, spending himself in me with one last thrust of his hips. He holds himself deep inside me, arms straining. "Say it," he demands, the tremor in his voice betraying his emotions.

"I'm yours," I agree because it's true. It's so true. I can't imagine my life without him, my big, strong, tender-hearted guy.

John lowers himself to my side, slipping out of my body. He keeps one arm and one leg draped over me, pinning me beneath him.

"I was thinking," he says, rolling to his back after we catch our breath. He takes me with him, and now I'm half-draped across his big body. It's bliss. Sticky, sated bliss.

"We could put the sofa there, across from the fireplace."

I nod, running my fingers through the smattering of damp hair on his chest. "Good place for it. But we're not keeping your hideous sectional."

John moves his head to peer at me. "Why? What's wrong with my couch?"

I snort. "Seriously? It looks like solidified baby vomit."

He seems to think for a moment. "Okay, you're right about that. But yours isn't much better."

He's not wrong there. "So, we get something new?"

He smiles, laugh-lines crinkling. "Yeah, something new."

"Something ours," I say, my words a whisper as I study his face. He looks so happy.

"Yeah ours," he agrees, kissing the top of my head. "I love you, Nightingale."

And, fuck. Those words, so easily given, are music to my ears. I feel lightheaded, woozy with delight, but safe in his arms.

"I love you too." I really do.

And – miracle of miracles – I'm not scared of getting lost in him. Quite the opposite, really, because I know John is staying.

I'm finally home.

ACKNOWLEDGMENTS

I have to thank Susan Scott Shelley and Roan Parrish for talking me down off the ledge. It gave me the kick I needed to get back on the writing horse.

Also, big thanks to Dena Heilik, Mary Calmes, and Jeff Adams for their Frankie & Johnny love. I wrote this story in a vacuum and never expected anyone else to love these boys as much as I do.

As always, my eternal love and gratitude to Mr. X for indulging my musical explorations.

∾

ABOUT THE AUTHOR

Xio Axelrod is a *USA TODAY* Bestselling author of love stories, contemporary romance and (what she likes to call) strange, twisted tales.

Xio grew up in the music industry and began recording at a young age. When she isn't writing stories, she can be found in the studio, writing songs, or performing on international stages (under a different, not-so-secret name of course).

She lives in Philadelphia with one full-time husband and several part-time cats.

ALSO BY XIO

When Frankie Meets Johnny

Originally published in volume two of the Love Is All anthology!

Scottish ex-pat Frankie Llewellyn lives and breathes music. Working late nights at WKMP, a radio station in suburban Philadelphia, he can play what he wants, sleep in every morning, and no one gives him any grief. No one but his most recent ex-boyfriend. Frankie is a serial monogamist, but after this latest break-up, he's worried he'll end up alone with nothing but his records to keep him warm at night.

When the station hires someone to do some much-needed renovations, Frankie is horrified to find out the work will be done during his overnight shift. But it makes the most sense, so he's resolved to take one for the team. After he meets the mysterious contractor, a gorgeous, lumberjack of a man named John Burton, Frankie decides it may not be such a hardship after all.

John is reserved, and a bit mysterious. Quite the contrast to Frankie's drama-filled life. But, as their friendship grows, John's quiet presence has Frankie singing a new song.

Fast Forward (an Alt Er Love novella)

As a nineteen-year-old, wunderkind doctoral candidate, Ian Waters had little interest in social interaction. Books were his companions, and that had suited him just fine. Then a hurricane named Jessen Sørensen blew into his life, throwing Ian off his axis.

On the cusp of rock stardom, Jessen had burned brightly, and Ian had fallen heart-first under his spell. But Ian soon learned he was only a temptation, a pit stop on the road to the rocker's dreams, and Jessen was gone as quickly as he'd come. Ian buried his heartache in academia, the only home he'd ever known.

When Ian encounters Jessen at a party, the seven-year separation seems insurmountable. There's too much pain, too much distrust. But Jessen declares he has a new dream, and that's a life with Ian.